T0114365

Contents

"The Black Gloves"

"**G**arage Sale! Yard Sale! Flea Market!" Well what is that all about? It simply means I love these things, places or whatever you call them. You have probably seen or heard of the bumper sticker that says, "Warning! I brake for Garage Sales." Well I need one of those on my van! Now that this foundation is established, beware if you are following too close behind me. Actually I have a couple of shopping bags in my van especially for that purpose. However, the following misadventure will definitely make me reconsider the things I buy—especially when I get strange "vibes" about it.

This is rather a long tale so please sit back and get comfortable as I tell you all about it.

I got an early start that day because my "to do list" was unusually long. Getting groceries was on the list and I hate that kind of shopping. No choice since we both like to eat and eat—too much I might add.

Suddenly my eyes noticed an orange sign. No one was in back of me, so I was able to slow down and read it. Sure enough, there it was! A bright orange sign with bold black letters stating, Estate Sale Today Only! Naturally, I quickly turned that direction.

"Wow!"—I exclaimed out loud, "How lucky can I get?" I figured I would be early enough to beat some of the market people there. I'm not one of "those"— but a person might think so if they saw my house.

My husband, Bill, has told me several times that I'm a pack rat and easy prey for a SALE sign. I laugh and try to deny it—but he's right. At least once a year I have a garage sale with some of the things that I just had to have. My only other option would be to open up a shop of my own—so maybe I am a "market person" at heart.

As I followed the signs for a few blocks, I was thinking, "Could be some fine collectibles for sale since these houses are extra nice."

The scene started changing abruptly into a much older neighborhood with the style of homes being from the 1940's. I contemplated turning around and continuing with my day as planned, when the orange sign stopped at a rusty but beautiful iron gate. It was wide open, so in I went.

There were so many huge trees and plants that I could only see sections of a large white frame house. As I drove down the winding driveway, I might add with some hesitation, the house began to take shape. It was a two and a half story structure, probably built in the early 1900's. As far as I could tell it didn't look too run down.

After parking I sat there for a few minutes thinking, "I'm here so I need to go inside just in case someone is watching as I wouldn't want to appear rude." For some reason, the house seemed a little foreboding.

What the heck, with my shopping bag in hand I bravely walked up to the old wooden porch.

There was only one car and a pickup truck in front, so I surmised there could not be many customers. Most likely one of the vehicles belonged to the people having the sale. The front door was propped open so I stepped inside. The only greeting I got was the musty smell of a place that had been closed up for many years. Quickly I glanced around the foyer and large living room and wondered where the owners or sales people were. For some reason I had a sad and empty feeling about this place.

The hardwood floors still had a little shine on them and scattered about were several fine Oriental type area rugs. Overall the furniture in this room appeared quite nice, but I didn't have space for anything very large.

I asked myself, "How could I be so lucky to be one of the first people here? Odd but then it's odd to have a sale in the middle of the week. Odder still that no one met me at the door. Definitely not professionally run."

I always have a strange feeling when I go to an estate sale, it's almost like I am invading someone's life and they are not present to protect their possessions. Guess it is like the saying, "You can't take it with you," but nonetheless, it is a little sad. It seems like most of the estate sales I have been to look pretty picked over by the time the doors open to the public. To me this is a good sign that says, the person or persons who lived there had a loving family and friends who appreciated and had room for some of their material memories. Of course, having room for is the big problem.

The sound of footsteps brought me back to reality as a nicely dressed, elderly lady came through the doorway. She reminded me of a dear aunt of mine that had passed on. Yes, Aunt L always dressed so proper and even wore hose in the summertime—as this lady probably does. As she came nearer I could smell the sweet scent of perfume, and I think it was the same kind my aunt wore. When I looked into her expressionless eyes and she spoke, the similarity ended.

She said, "We wish to get rid of these things as soon as possible, so if you find something, just state what you will give for it." Her next comment was, "Go upstairs if you wish—I am staying down here to have a cup of tea. She hurried from the room, I guess towards the kitchen.

Well that was certainly a different sales pitch. Frankly I don't like that kind of sale because I never know what most things are worth and I don't want to hurt someone's feelings or embarrass myself.

Casually I looked around at the interesting assortment of glassware, books and other small articles. There were two figurines and a book that I especially wanted, so I carefully placed them in my shopping bag. I jotted down some of items that I would consider, if the lady agreed to my offer. There were so many dusty, but impressive things to look at in this one room alone that I hardly knew where to start, so I decided to check out the rest of the house and then work my way back here.

The stern faced woman came through the door about the time I was going out and we nearly collided. Thank goodness we didn't as she was carrying a tray with a pot of steaming hot tea. She sat it down on the coffee table then eased herself into one of the colorful overstuffed chairs that faced the front door. I got a strong feeling that she did not like being in this house at all.

As I walked down the hall I came to the stairway. I could hear a man and woman arguing on the next level up, and though I couldn't understand what they were saying, the tone sounded quite serious. That would be embarrassing to walk into a scene like that so I turned to go in another direction. A young couple and another elderly lady that favored the one I had talked with in the living room came towards me. I am thinking that they are without a doubt sisters and owners of this old home. We greeted each other and I commented about all the nice furnishings that were for sale.

The young lady said, "It must be super sad to let all this great stuff go to strangers."

With a strange tone in her voice the older lady sharply remarked, "Sometimes it's sadder to view things, so it is better to get them out of sight."

"Well that is something to think about," I answered.

I asked the older lady if the person I had met coming in was her sister. Her answer was a simple, "Yes."

My next question brought a shocked expression to her face as I casually asked, "I would like to look upstairs but wasn't sure if it would it be all right since I heard some pretty angry voices coming from up there."

"There is NO ONE upstairs—perhaps it was sounds of someone outside," was her reply.

Well I didn't go for that explanation since this house sits on a large lot and is back from all the others. I reasoned it was most likely some customers wanting the same object so I started up the old stairs to check it out. No sneaking up these creaking steps even the carpet runner couldn't hide that. To me that just gives character to older homes. There were a few dark stains on the carpet that no one had bothered to remove, but I guess in past times, they had no good stain removers.

Several large portraits (I supposed family members) were arranged in a stair step design which is a common practice. I felt as if their eyes were following me with each step I took. This is nothing unusual either—but it still gives me a creepy feeling. I expect most people will admit that this has happened to them before.

In the first picture there was a couple staring at me with piercing eyes and stern faces. It's hard to tell but I would guess them to be near eighty years old.

Following those two was an unsmiling, domineering looking man. Next was of a woman with two young girls who were probably her daughters. All were dressed very conservatively and had little expression on their faces. The woman looked sad or perhaps ill or, maybe just a no nonsense person. Here I go judging people again! Most likely there was little happiness in their lives to be smiling about, specially, if that last guy was the husband and father.

With the next step up I smiled at this fellow, because he was of the "Clark Gable" type—downright handsome! His portrait was in an ornate gold frame while the lower ones were in plain black.

As I ascended a few more steps, a draft of cold air hit me. I jumped and nearly dropped my shopping bag. Loudly I said, "Yikes! What the heck caused that?" They didn't have air conditioning only ceiling fans as far as I could tell. Looking around, I saw no visible place for the cold air to come from. "Never mind" I tell myself, "This old house could use some fresh air but not in just one cold blast like that."

"Wow!"—My mouth flew open at the last portrait. Inside a richly carved, gold frame was a very sexy looking lady with blond hair cascading over her shoulders. She wore a low-cut black satin dress with matching long black gloves that were trimmed with rhinestones. Perhaps she was the wife or a girlfriend of the good looking man next to her. Glancing down the stairs, I was glad no one was watching me as I studied their relatives.

Silently I scolded myself, "What the heck—I'm not here to analyze these people. I'm here to buy something interesting, so get on with 'the program' Karen!"

There were several rooms upstairs, but I really didn't have time to check them all out so I decided on two of them. You know the "let your intuition be your guide" thing. Gut feeling or whatever!

Suddenly a harsh jumble of words came from the room I was about to enter, so I stopped for a moment.

I thought to myself—"What the heck, I have just as much right to be in there as they do. If they don't like it they can take their arguing outside."

With full resolve I walked into the room. It was strikingly different with almost everything decorated in red and black. However, the most astonishing thing was—there were no people in this room! Where could they be? My hearing is good and I know the voices were coming from this room.

"Hmm!" I said aloud, "Very puzzling!"—Oh well, maybe there are a few spooks in this old house. That would answer some of my questions.

My plan was to make up my mind on certain items and get out of there as quickly as possible. I turned around to take a better look at the room and my eyes nearly "popped out." The same sexy blond by the stairs was staring at me again. This time she was wearing nothing but those long, black gloves with a small red pillow covering her most private parts. She was certainly proud of herself and didn't mind flaunting her body in front of some artist or whoever walked into this room.

The portrait was hanging above an old but beautiful black iron bed with fancy rose and cupid designs. I noticed a cute red pillow trimmed with black fringe at the foot of the bed and realized it was the same one in the painting.

I'm thinking, "This is really cute, I'm sure I can find a place to display it, and what a nice conversation piece it will make." I put it in my shopping bag between the two figurines for protection.

As I turned to leave I spotted the same black satin gloves draped over the iron bedpost. Undoubtedly these gloves were extra special to the blond lady since she was wearing them in both portraits. I just couldn't resist picking them up and examining them. Believe it or not, there was a long blond hair twisted around one of the rhinestones. I could see why she was so proud of them—they were really unique.

I heard myself say, "Man, I have got to try these on just for the heck of it." I put my shopping bag down on the bed and pulled the long gloves on. "Great, they seemed to be made for my hands!" At the same time there was an inner voice trying to tell me, "But you never go anywhere to wear something this fancy." I should have listened! I walked over to the old fashioned dresser—you know the kind that has the small mirrors that fold out on the sides. Arranged "just so so" on the dusty surface were at least a dozen beautifully shaped bottles of perfume. I was tempted to try or at least smell some, but I didn't. There were other items a lady might use to make herself irresistible to the guys, especially a sexy chick like the blond in the two pictures. It wasn't hard to imagine her standing in front of this dresser trying to decide which fragrance to choose. I stood looking into the mirrors from all angles admiring the black gloves that I was still wearing.

I heard myself say, "I'm going to buy them, no matter what they cost." I was puzzled at my words of determination which were unlike anything I would normally think or say.

No doubt, I was definitely acting weird. Like I mentioned before, I seldom talk to myself, but since stepping onto this property I can no longer brag about that. Taking the fascinating gloves off, I placed them in my shopping bag with the other items. I turned to leave and gave a final glance into the bedroom. My eyes played a trick on me because I thought I saw a woman with blond hair in one of the small mirrors. My goose bumps were starting to get goose bumps on them and I felt like other eyes were watching me. "Impossible," I reasoned because no one else was in this room, at least in solid form.

I hurried to the stairs and as I passed by the glamorous lady in the big gold frame, I felt a cold, prickly sensation around my whole body. There she was with a crooked smile just staring at me taking away her black gloves. PARANOIA here I come!

As carefully and fast as possible, I got down to the first floor and into the living room where the other humans were. Humans with flesh that is!

The young couple was almost finished with their transactions and, judging by the long list on the table, they must be furnishing their whole house or apartment. Under normal circumstances this would be costing them a considerable amount of money— however, I don't consider this a normal sale by normal people.

The two sisters almost smiled as the young man handed them the check. From the comments made by 'sister number one' earlier, I'm thinking they are glad to get rid of these things—period! She told the young couple that she thought they had chosen wisely and should have no problems with any of it. With a thanks and, we will be back with a truck this evening, they were out the door.

"Well, what did you end up with Madam," was the question sister number one asked me. I took the book, figurines, pillow and last of all the black gloves out of my bag and placed them on the table.

You would have thought I threw a poisonous snake at them from their expressions. Puzzled I asked them, "What on earth is wrong?"

The sister I had met last spoke up sharply, "Why would anyone want the black gloves that cheap hussy wore?"

The other woman quickly apologized for her sister's remarks. She turned to her sister and said, "Now, Adella, she didn't know her. Since she is dead, we must try to forget all about that horrible person."

Her response was a statement not a question. "Oh, is she really dead!" From my brief encounter I was inclined to think Adella was right. However, I certainly did not want to take part in this strange drama that I was unwittingly getting involved in.

Trying to calm the situation down I said, "I'm sorry if I did something to upset you ladies, I just assumed the gloves were for sale."

Adella's face was twisted by hate as she blurted out, "They are as well as everything else in this house, Madam. In fact you can have that gold-digging tramp's picture wearing her black gloves and her evil smile."

I blushed and said, "Thanks, but no thanks, not even with the gold frame." Wow, I told myself, you need to leave before she has a stroke! Quickly I added, in the calmest voice I could muster, "How much do I owe you?"

In a sad voice the sister number one sighed, "Whatever you wish my dear." I gave her a fifty dollar bill and asked if that was sufficient.

She replied, "Yes, but would it be too much trouble for you to give me a check instead?" Almost in a whisper she replied, "I have a good reason."

How strange can things get?— A person wanting a check instead of cash?—What the heck, I thought, and wrote the check so quickly that

I hoped she would be able to read it. Gathering up my things, I hurried out the front door. What a nut house and spooky to boot!

Once safely in my car, I had to take one more peek at my new treasures—especially those notorious black gloves. As I drove through the rusty gate I was surprised to see the Estate sale sign was no longer there. Hmm—that was quick sale! I backtracked to the street where I had originally seen it, and noticed someone had removed that sign also. No wonder they didn't have more customers. Guess they were not so anxious to get rid of things after all.

As I drove into the Grocery Mart parking lot, I exclaimed out loud, "Back to some normal shopping. I've had more than enough of the abnormal kind to last me a long time."

I glanced into the back seat and, yes, there were MY black gloves on top of the red pillow; it wasn't just a silly dream. Suddenly I had the urge to shop for a cocktail dress that would go with them. Why, should have been my question, since my husband never takes me anyplace where that would be appropriate. Without considering the "why of it"—I wheeled my vehicle around and headed to one of the most sophisticated and expensive shops in town. Buzzing into a handicapped parking spot, I gently picked up the black gloves and casually walked up to the door.

All eyes seemed to be on me as I entered the shop. I guess my jeans and plain shirt looked out of place. I suddenly realized where I was and it was the whole me that was out of place.

As I turned to leave, a sexy dressed young lady said to me, "Madam would you care to see something that would go with your gloves?"

I glanced down at the long black gloves in my hand almost as if I didn't know they were there. Too weird! Well, I thought—why else would anyone be carrying or wearing gloves of this type unless they were trying to match them up with something.

I stammered, "Ah—ah sorry, I am in the wrong place." Needless to say everyone in the store gave me strange looks as I left—but not as strange as I felt.

When I noticed where I had parked, I knew I was definitely acting weird. Possessed would be a better description! As quickly as possible I drove back to the grocery store, and I'm thankful I had a list or there's no telling what I would have bought. Lucky I didn't run into anyone with my shopping cart as I hurried up and down the aisles. No label detail reading today!

While driving home I declared to myself, "I need to get home and get my head on straight—the sooner the better!"

After unloading the grocery bags, I carried my infamous estate sale treasures (not sure about those black gloves) into the guestroom. This room is furnished totally with antiques, iron bed, etc. It is seldom used so that's where I stash things till I can figure out a more permanent place for them.

When my husband came in from work and dinner was over, I had to tell him about my crazy day. Much of it was hard to explain but he patiently listened with many, "you're kidding" and "no way" remarks.

We sat there in silence for awhile just trying to think things out. Suddenly Bill had a revelation and exclaimed, "It is all because of that blond woman and her black gloves! Maybe she was a greedy hussy like the old sisters said."

I agreed one hundred percent on that and decided it would best if I put the gloves into a box and figure out what to do with them later. How could something so pretty have such bad vibes?

A few days later I went into the guestroom to box up the items that seemed to represent the lady with no name—other than the blond hussy.

Taking a step back I cried out, "How can this be?" The black gloves were neatly draped over the bedpost and the red pillow had found 'its' place at the end of the bed just as they had been in the room at the estate sale. I knew this was not where I had put them.

There was no one to hear me but I spoke loudly, "I don't like this one bit and if Bill thinks this is funny, he won't for long!" I threw the gloves and pillow into the box and pushed them under the bed. Still angry with my tricky husband, I phoned him at his work place.

In his normal voice he said, "Hey Karen, what's up?"

"You know, you dirty rat—that was NOT funny!"

With total surprise in his voice he said, "What on earth are you screeching about?"

"Now, Bill, don't play dumb with me, you know very well," was my answer.

"Please" he said, "I don't have a clue! Tell me why you are so upset, you know I'm not the type to play jokes."

A little more calmly I said, "I'm sorry to have wrongly accused you Bill, I should have known better." I told him about the gloves and red pillow being moved from where I had put them, so I figured he was the only person who could have done that.

He asked, "You sure you didn't forget doing that?"

"Certain—? Of course I'm certain."

After a few moments Bill said, "Pretty or not, you must get rid of those crazy things."

No arguing that point as I knew he was right. But how, was the question?

My comments were; "I can't give them away or throw them in the trash because some other unsuspecting person might be cursed by them." "Cursed? Hmm—I didn't know that word was in my vocabulary. I'll let you go, Bill, and please forgive me for being so harsh with you."

He said, "Don't worry, Hon, if you had played a trick like that on me, I would have fussed at you big time."

I walked from the room with firm resolve that I would find a way to do away with those gloves and pillow.

The next few days were so busy with meetings and other obligations that I had put the blond hussy's prized possessions "on the back burner," so to speak. Maybe that would literally be a good idea!

It was our first evening at home with nothing special to do but relax so I figured this would be a good time to read some from the book I had gotten at the estate sale. I had left it on the dresser in the guestroom. As I entered the room I let out a scream!

Bill came running to my rescue calling, "What's wrong?"

All I could do was point at the bed. The red pillow was back at the foot of the bed and those Black Gloves were hanging over the bedpost as before. Tears filled my eyes as I looked down at the floor where my once beautiful figurines lay smashed. Some cruel unseen hands had broken their heads off! My book was torn to shreds and scattered about the room.

Bill hollered out, "What—the—crap?"

"EVIL! They are evil," was my cry!

Bill was comforting as he guided me back to the living room and said, "Try to calm down, we will beat this thing!"

I sobbed, "How can we get rid of her ghost, or whatever it is?"

Bill commented, "She must have been a witch to be able to reach out from her grave and do things like this is all I can say. Karen, try to relax. I'll clean-up the room and put her fancy black gloves and red pillow in a tote box." With an assuring tone he said, "Believe me, there will be so many bungee cords on it Houdini wouldn't be able to get out."

In about thirty minutes Bill came through on his way to the garage saying, "I'm putting this in the trunk of your car, and I'll deal with it when I get home tomorrow evening."

Needless to say we didn't sleep well that night.

The next morning after Bill left for work I busied myself working in the flower garden in front. To me this is good therapy and I was in need of a "heavy dose" of that. I silently said a prayer that this crazy situation would be over soon. About that time the sound of footsteps coming down the driveway snapped me back to reality.

My mailman with his usual big smile and cheery voice said, "Hey, Ms. Hudson, how's your day going?"

"Well, I have definitely seen better ones—but I'm sure it will improve," was my answer.

He had a puzzled look on his face but he didn't ask what the problem was.

This envelope was too large for your box, so you get special delivery. If I see you tomorrow, I hope to see a big smile."

"Thanks," was my reply as he handed me the rest of the mail and went on his way whistling a happy tune.

I figured the brown envelope was just junk, probably another calendar. As I took my work gloves off, I noticed there was no return address and centered so perfectly was my name written in old-fashioned script. With a nervous feeling I opened the large envelope. This was going to take serious reading, so I went into the house. It was stuffed full and had extra postage stamps to ensure it got delivered. The first line told me it was from one of the Estate sale sisters. Adella was probably still upset with me for wanting those black gloves and pillow.

At least I know now why the calmer sister wanted a check. She wanted my address so she could write to me.

"Why would she want to write me?" was my next question. Enough suspense!

The handwriting was pretty but appeared a little shaky. She was probably nervous about writing to a stranger. I poured myself a cup of coffee and began reading the long letter. It was like a well-written short story, full of intrigue, mystery and terribly sad. It certainly cleared up most of my questions. Pieces of the "puzzle" started falling into place and it was NOT a pretty picture.

Here's the letter that I received—word for word.

Dear Mrs. Hudson. My first name is Sara and it is best you do not know my last name or where I live now.

You deserve an explanation regarding the harsh words that were said to you, and any other strange things that may have happened while you were at our estate sale.

Incidentally, in the last forty years we have had very little to do with our old home-place. We hired different men to keep-up the yard, paid necessary taxes and had it painted once. That poor man told us he had a hard time finishing the job because it felt like someone was watching him all the time. He called it the "Willies." Adella and I knew exactly what he was talking about. Four different times we returned, but were always greeted with an ominous evil presence. We felt sure it was not just our imagination. With that said, I shall get back to the part that concerns you, my dear.

Again, please forgive my sister Adella and me for the rude and unladylike manner in which we treated you. It was totally unacceptable! I felt obliged to explain our situation and that of the people who were a part of the old house you came to. We call it the Sad House, because I feel it was always that way for us. From the look on your face when you came downstairs, I think you sensed something sad or unnatural about it also.

However, the main reason I'm writing this letter to you is out of concern. Since you bought two of Her favorite things, I was afraid you might have experienced ill effects from them... I pray not!

It is hard to find a starting point for my "tale of woe," but I shall try by telling you something about the people who lived in our Sad House.

I'm sure you noticed the row of portraits as you went up the stairway. The last one was nothing but a gold digging tramp. As my letter unfolds, you will understand why we are still very bitter about her. She was definitely not a family member even though she schemed to be.

To this day, even though she and Max (her partner in crime) died many years ago, she still tries to be in control. No one can understand how this is possible, but there is too much evidence of her evilness lingering there to deny. Some of the strange events that have occurred there revolve around those beastly black satin gloves and her fancy pillow. As I said, this is the main reason I am writing you. Sorry, I lost my train of thought, but you may need to know this information.

The first picture you came to was of our grandparents on Father's side of the family. They were, as the portrait reveals them to be, very serious minded folks. Both passed away when Adella and I were in our teens.

Before I continue with the people in the portraits, the following information will help you understand our situation better.

Between our grandfather and father, we were not allowed to take part in anything other than church activities and some school things. It was a treat just to go shopping for food with mother.

Father would say, "We have enough glitter around here already, just get what is necessary."

I'm sure you noticed some of the beautiful glassware and fine rugs; these were inherited from my mother's side of the family. The two figurines you bought were hers.

Grandmother and Mother were always quiet and never spoke up for their rights or ours. The men were what you young people nowadays would call control freaks. "God rest their souls!"

Father was the only child out of eight to survive to adulthood, so that alone had to account for some bitterness and many sad times.

His parents were the original owners of Sad House and, since he was their only child, Father would naturally inherit everything. He told us several times that we had no worries in event of his death. You see, he was a very "matter of fact" person about everything. We just wanted to be happy in the present time.

Adella and I were proud of the house and pretty grounds but we seldom had friends over to enjoy it. Grandfather and Father were in business together, but I will not say what kind. Pardon me for being so secretive.

The second picture is of our father. Third in line is Mother, Adella and me. Sorry to say, we do not appear happy or at ease and for good reasons.

Father's thoughts were outdated by forty years at least. We females were expected to keep the "men folk" happy and everything in perfect order around that big house. There was never a thank you. Father often said, "Just be glad you have a roof over your head."

We were sad people in a sad old house! This was the way things were for the next several years. One day there was a change, but not for the good!

Now the next two pictures most definitely should not be there with our family. If they weren't so heavy we would have moved them—if we had dared!

She and Max hung them shortly before our father died.

The blond hussy said, "A prominent position and nothing less than gold leaf frames will do for us—we deserve to be here!"

Forgive my wandering mind as I find myself getting ahead of the events as they took place. With that explained, I'll get back to introducing the people.

The fourth picture is or was Max Darbey, some distant kin on Grandfather's side—so he said. Not long after Grandfather had died he appeared at the front door and asked if he might stay awhile. Of course, Mother and Father welcomed him since he had told them he claimed to be kin.

He was very charming at first, but we found out later that it was only a disguise. It was exciting to have a handsome fellow like him in our house. We enjoyed being teased and couldn't keep from laughing as he tussled our hair around. This made father's face red and even sterner.

I think if we had been allowed a more normal life, we would have had boyfriends and not been so enchanted with Max.

Sorry, those remarks have nothing to do with my letter of warning. When I think back on things, I get emotional all over again.

The last picture is of Her wearing her long black gloves and looking like a glamour queen.

Mrs. Hudson, as you see, I have scattered remarks throughout this letter about this blond hussy. Sorry to say they get much worse, and you will soon know what a horrible person the previous owner of the black gloves was—or still is.

Mother and Father diplomatically asked Max several times just how long he planned to stay. He would just laugh and say "You people are so hospitable I hate to leave."

However, one day he did leave but was back the next week with a fancy dressed young lady.

Proudly he said, "This is my sweetie. Her name is Mazie."

My heart seemed to drop within me because I had a crush on Max. I'm surprised I knew what a crush was. Adella was probably the only other person that saw this.

Now the tale of "real woe" begins.

I imagine you could tell what a haughty person she was by just looking at her portraits. We soon found that was one of her better traits. She flaunted her phony smile, flashy clothes, and (I hate to admit it) her well built body. Men seemed hypnotized by her and sorry to say, one was our father!

This is when Adella and I made a vow to never trust any man, much less marry one.

Max proudly showed her off like she was the Queen of Sheba. Sometimes rather than speak, she would just flash her fake smile and laugh and flutter her long eyelashes.

Sorry Mrs. Hudson, as you can tell I am still very bitter just thinking of her... Back to the sordid story!

Poor gentle Mother! "When would they leave?" That's the question we heard Mother ask Father several times, yet he paid her little mind.

If he liked such a fancy dresser, why did he want HIS females to dress so plain? That was a question Adella and I discussed often.

Being a man we guessed he couldn't resist the attention she gave him. However, we felt certain they were never physically involved. He would never let 'it' go that far.

Around this time is when Max and Mazie started arguing a lot. You probably noticed that we never referred to her as Mazie, just hussy (behind her back, of course). She treated us like her servants, so we figured she didn't deserve a proper name. Mother, Adella and I saw them as uninvited guest and wanted them to go. However, we had no say—until it was too late.

I'm truly sorry to be burdening you with this personal information, but I didn't know what else to do, and writing this letter has made me feel somewhat better. I am relieved to tell someone because Adella and I never told anyone the tragic things that happened in our early life. Why should we?

Praise the Lord, after some time we did find contentment and are now leading productive lives. We kept our oath to each other and never got married. Now back to my story.

Mother tried to ignore the hussy flirting with her husband and the loud fights she had with Max, till she could stand it no longer. Mother told the hussy that she and Max would have to move out immediately.

Mazie answered sharply, "It will take us time to find a place and besides I'm not sure everyone wants us to leave."

Mother's health began to deteriorate shortly after that episode. The doctor thought at first it was a common stomach problem, but none of the normal treatments did any good. During this time Adella and I noticed the hussy was more attentive to Mother, which was out of character for her. This alone made us suspicious of her, as she seemed so patronizing. She would serve Mother hot tea and cookies on a regular basis. Oddly she wore those silly black gloves which were so out of place. We figured she must be ashamed of her hands. One day I noticed a white powdery substance on them and asked her what it was, and she casually said, "Oh, flour I guess." She never did any cooking so how could that be?

We did not trust her in the least and I told her to stay away from our mother because we could care for her ourselves.

Father began showing more love and concern for Mother and that put a weak smile on her face. This was encouraging. We thought she was gaining back her strength, but our dear mother passed away in her sleep not long after that.... Such a sad time!

Just two weeks later that brazen hussy resumed her flirting with our father quite openly. Thankfully he did not respond favorably to her.

She and Max started having harsh words with each other on a regular basis and not caring who heard them. At night their angry voices could be heard coming from their room. Yes, it had become their room it seemed! The few words we could make out were—Max saying, "Your idea!" Her screaming, "Someone had to!" Max yelling, "No!" She screeched, "Soon be ours. Max saying, "An accident?" In a demanding voice the hussy said, "Your turn, you wimp!" As you can imagine, these words made no sense – at the time. Sometimes Max filled in the spaces with an occasional curse word. However, there was one sentence we understood clearly. It was, "No—that is going too far!"

We figured they were planning a way to get their hands on our father's money or maybe he was just jealous of the attention Mazie was giving our father.

Only two months had passed since our mother's death when our father apparently died of a heart attack. Adella found him slumped over his desk in the reading room with a book in one hand and pen in the other. Our poor dear father had been so sad since Mother died; we were afraid he partly blamed himself. It was a terribly sad time for my sister and me, but we managed to get through it and make proper arrangements for father. We were in our early twenties when this took place so a friend of father's advised us on matters. Max wanted to be present but we refused his help. At this point we thought he might just be trying to help himself to part of the inheritance. Adella and I were the only legal heirs but, since Father's Last Will and Testament could not be found as proof, it would take longer to finalize.

We knew our next priority was to get Max and his troublesome woman out of our house as quickly as possible. Max informed us that our father had told him he could stay as long as he liked. We did not believe this for one minute!

With no hesitation Adella stormed back at him, "We own this house now so you two need to pack-up right away."

I stood firm with Adella and added, "We have had nothing but trouble since you two moved in here." Sorry, here I go again saying more than I should. Please forgive me.

We thought we were going to need a court order to get them out because almost a week had passed since we had issued the ultimatum to leave, and they just ignored us.

One evening as Adella and I sat in the living room, we were startled by loud sounds coming from upstairs. As usual it was from our unwanted houseguests. We got up and walked into the hall just in time to see them struggling near the top steps. Max had blood running down his face. Apparently this evil woman had hit him in the head with the iron candleholder that she clinched in her gloved hand. Her prized black gloves, of course. Max grabbed her by the neck and they both tumbled all the way down the stairs. Their twisted bodies and glazed eyes told us they must be dead.

We stared in disbelief as this horrible nightmare unfolded before our eyes. When we came to our senses, I called the police. The ambulance came but there was nothing the doctor could do except pronounce them dead. After pictures were taken of the death scene, their bodies were carried away.

Almost in a state of shock, we told the sheriff about the horrible scene we had witnessed. He expressed his sympathy regarding that and all the other sad events we had gone through. The sheriff gently patted us on the back and suggested a vacation away from this place would be good for us, and then he and his investigating team left.

We were still trembling as we hugged each other. What a frightful thing! The house had an eerie quietness about it and we knew there no was no way we could spend that night there. In fact we discussed the possibility that we might never feel at ease living in our Sad house.

We hated to walk up the stairs where that terrible thing had just happened, but we needed to pack some clothes and other items from our bedrooms.

At the foot of the stairs we felt a swirl of cold air coming from sources unknown. I prayed to God to keep us strong and free from harm as we climbed the stairs. We couldn't do this as quickly as we would have liked because there were puddles of coagulating blood on the carpet in several places. It was all we could do to keep from throwing up. Believe me, it was so sickening!

We made it to our rooms and filled our suitcases as fast as we could. Adella suggested we should come back the next day when it was light to get what else we needed. At least we had plenty of money to carry us through this horrible nightmare.

As we hurried down the hall to the stairs, I glanced into their room half expecting to see her blond sneering face. What I did see made me scream... "Her gloves! Her black gloves were hanging on the bedpost. How could this be when she was wearing them when the ambulance took her body away?" That was an unanswerable question!

Mrs. Hudson, I'm sure you understand now the importance of getting rid of those black gloves, and as quickly as possible.

Now back to our story. Without further delay we carried our suitcases down the stairs and carefully stepped over that sickening blood. Again the cold air brushed my cheek.

After spending a restless night in a nearby motel, we decided to wait until we got home to eat breakfast since we had food there.

Thank goodness we had learned to drive, and even that was done in secret.

Weather wise it was a beautiful day, but heavy clouds hung over our hearts. Driving through the pretty iron gates everything looked normal and peaceful. My—my, how looks can deceive!

We walked directly into the kitchen not daring to look towards the staircase. Our breakfast was prepared quickly, put on a tray and carried to our favorite spot in the reading room. In fact, it was at the desk where Father had died. I reached over to move the book he was reading on that sad day. A folded paper and white envelope fell out. The envelope was from a law firm in town. It contained his Last Will and Testament. That was a relief, as it would simplify all things.

I unfolded the paper and it was from father. Neither of us could keep the tears from flowing as I read it. It was a letter dated the same day he died so he must have had a premonition of his impending death. Mainly he wrote how much he had always loved mother and us above all else. He then apologized for not sending Max and his girlfriend, Mazie away when mother had asked him to. Father said at times, he felt like he was under some sort of spell, but had come to his senses before their mother died— but then it was too late.

His handwriting wavered as he told what that evil hussy suggested to him. He wrote, "When your mother was sick she came to me saying she would get rid of Max, and when your mother was dead we could be together. Her words and implications made me sick to death."

Adella and I screamed out similar words, that wicked, gold digging hussy! Perhaps she DID have something to do with mother's death as we had suspected.

Father's next words were, "I will tell them they must move out as soon as possible." The next line was scrawled out rapidly, "Someone coming! Finish later! Must hide this!"

Evidently he had stuffed the letter into the book just before "that someone" came into the room—. No more was ever written.

Stunned we realized we had been living in the house with possible murders.

The doorbell rang, bringing us back to the present. It was the Sheriff.

He said, "Ladies, this letter was in Max Darbey's wallet and addressed to you. Would you mind telling me what it says as it may clear up some things?" I asked him to read it because neither of us wanted to touch it.

Mrs. Hudson, I am also copying that note 'word for word' for you. As terrible as it is, I can't leave this out because it explains other tragic details.

The note was dated the day after Father was found dead. It read: "If you are reading this before we moved away, I am probably dead. Please forgive me for bringing Mazie into your home. I never knew she was cruel enough to do what she did. I only planned to 'get in good' with your father and mother so they might add me to their will.

Brace yourselves as I tell you just how cold-blooded and devious she is. The night your father died she excitedly told me she had solved part of the problem. I didn't know what she was referring to. That's when she told me that she had been gradually poisoning your mother, but since that was taking too long, she suffocated her with her red pillow while she was sleeping. Bluntly Mazie said, "She had to because she thought your mother was getting well." I stared at her in disbelief as she calmly stated, "Oh yes, I did the old guy in with a cup of strong coffee. Well, it did contain some harmless sleeping pills, she smirked. After all, I couldn't have him struggling as I put my pretty red pillow over his face. Now it's your turn to get rid of those prissy girls!"

I yelled at her calling her every vile thing I could think of.

She just said, "Do it and the whole place will be ours!"_

I called her a crazy devil and said we would both be sharing a bed of hot coals in Hell. Grabbing hold of her, I told her we were leaving as soon as possible. If looks could kill, I would have died on the spot.

The next day before she woke up, I wrote this letter, just in case she decided to 'do me in.' Sorry I'm so spineless, but I couldn't stand the thought of being in prison for life, so my plan is to run away. However, first I must figure some way to get Mazie away from you girls and your house.

Adella and Sara— I wish to God we had never come into your lives. Cousin, Max"

We were stunned and sick at our stomachs at the reading of these horrible details in Max's letter.

The Sheriff said, "I've never heard of a more cold-blooded person as this Mazie, but I best not call her what I really think of her in front of you ladies."

He strongly suggested we should take a long vacation from this terrible scene as quickly as possible. We agreed! The Sheriff said they would not need any further statements from us because the letter told them all they needed to know.

His last words were, "At least that damned pair checked out in a fitting way.—Excuse my language ladies."

After he left we sat there in a daze for a while just trying to decide what we should do. Most importantly—to just get away from this terrible place. I broke the silence by suggesting we should go to the tourist center today and see what they might recommend. Later that day Adella and I talked with an understanding lady who said she knew just the place we would find beautiful scenery, peace and not too many tourists. Arrangements were made to leave the next day.

Adella and I found Mother and Father's large suitcase and filled it with essentials needed for our trip.

We spent one more night at the motel then, drove back to our house early the next morning. I parked close to the front porch; we put our luggage, such as it was, on the bottom step, then I locked the car in the garage.

With luggage by our side, we waited for the taxi that would take us to the tour bus. Everything seemed so unreal as we sat there—so tense and quite.

Though the morning dampness seemed extra cold, there was no way we were waiting inside. Even out there it seemed invisible eyes were gazing at us... We never looked around!

Sorry, Mrs. Hudson for this long letter but I am almost finished.

We went on a two-month bus tour of the country, and it was just wonderful to be away from our Sad old House. Of course there is no way to rid oneself from the horrible thoughts and things that took place there, but for the first time in our lives, we felt free. It was wonderful.

However, we needed to face reality, so we went back home to see if we would be able to live in our old Sad house again.

The taxi driver dropped us off and was kind enough to carry some of our bags for us. He put them just inside the door. We thanked him and he drove off. Since we were so tired, I suggested we leave our bags there until we saw what took place.

"Well," Adella said, "Here we are again!"

There it stood looking quite lonely—but was it? I told her maybe we could do something worthwhile with it. Our town could use a museum— but not one possessed with evil... Sorry, but we had to give up on that idea.

We climbed the stairs trying not to think of what took place there— but to no avail. At the bottom and top of the stairs there was a cold tingling sensation that greeted us... It was just too much! Those memories would never go away any more than the dark bloodstains on the carpet. Nonetheless, we had decided to give it a try and spend the night there. We hurried up the stairs to our bedrooms. I quickly shut 'their' door as we passed by—making a point not to look in. Our rooms were separated by a bathroom, so we entered by way of mine, then quickly locked both doors leading into the hall. After a bit we said our good nights and I finally drifted off to sleep, but only to be awakened a short time later. In a state of terror, I cried out, "Oh no—their voices!" A jumble of angry words came from Max and the evil hussy's room. Adella and I nearly collided with each other as we ran to see if the other was hearing the sounds. Without a word we hurriedly dressed, grabbed our bags and left the house.

Back at the motel, we stretched out on our beds with a defeated feeling, and did more tossing and thinking than sleeping.

We awoke to a dreary morning, and though we didn't feel like eating, we knew we needed to keep our strength up... Remember, Mrs. Hudson, even though we were young ladies, we had learned to be strong.

Adella and I agreed there was no way we would ever stay in that house again. We needed to get rid of it—but we would not 'pawn' our ghost house off on some unsuspecting person. However, since there were so many nice furnishings we had no room for, we decided to have a one day estate sale —which we did.

Two days later I called a local mover and luckily they were able to meet us a couple of hours later. Back at the motel, we talked over what things we would need to set up living somewhere else. We would put those things in storage until we found a small house in one of the towns our tour had taken us. The climate would be warmer, and hopefully the people. Thoughts of that gave us hope.

Walking across the creaking porch and into the living room, we wondered if there were angry eyes watching us. I told my sister to remember, this was OUR house, not that ghostly pair'.

There were so many special things of mother and father's, and of course our own, that we had a hard time choosing what we would take. Things that had nothing whatsoever to do with that murdering hussy or Max!

As we walked up and down the hall, we ignored the closed door as best we could.

The movers came and did a good job securing our precious cargo into their large truck then taking it to a near-by storage building.

Please read this part carefully, Mrs. Hudson. We came up with a plan to permanently be rid of Sad House and Its unwanted GUEST and her belongings. We would burn it down! This is not for insurance because there is none. As you know it is not near other houses that could burn so we feel that will be safe enough. We have reasoned this out to the best of our ability and though it seems like a very drastic decision, we will do it. I pray you will not consider us crazy or bad people.

Now my dear, this would be the perfect way for you to rid yourself of those cursed black gloves and that horrible red pillow. If you are wise you will follow these instructions.

Put those items in a paper bag and place them on the front porch by 6:00 PM on Friday the 10th and we will take care of the rest.

Most sincerely, Sara"

I shook my head in disbelief as I finished her letter.

Those poor dear ladies have endured such horrible things for so long. Just thinking about how their parents died brought tears to my eyes. I agreed one hundred percent with what they had planned, and perhaps it was the only solution.

How on earth could two mild mannered ladies think such a thing up? My answer would have to be, desperation and determination.

They certainly needed closure regarding anything that represented that evil man and his murderous mistress.

Luckily it was only two days before the 10th... I hoped Bill would agree to the plan because he knew we needed to be rid of those black gloves and red pillow and this was better than any we had come up with.

When Bill came home from work I asked him to sit down and read the letter from the Estate ladies. His remarks and facial expressions were quite fitting considering the material he was reading. "What a damn shame! That's the most terrible thing that I have EVER heard of—and scary!" He said without hesitation, "It is imperative that we follow this Sara's instruction."

I said, "GREAT!"

We couldn't resist looking in the guestroom to be sure the gloves and pillow had not made their way back in there. Thank God they hadn't! We also checked in the trunk of my car and the tote box was still securely wrapped.

On Friday the 10th at five PM we were driving through the iron gates of the old "Sad house." Bill took the bungee cords off, and I quickly removed the red pillow and black gloves from the tote bag and stuffed them into a paper bag. Knowing their story, I could hardly stand to touch them.

Bill hurried onto the porch and placed the bag directly against the house and moved a pot plant against it so there was no possibility of it blowing away.

There were so many trees and bushes around the front part of the house, no one would have been able see him, but he kept looking around. He probably sensed the same unseen eyes peering at him that I did.

I said aloud, "Well—Blond Hussy, you have your black gloves and red pillow back—but not the way you planned."

Jumping in the car, Bill let out a sigh of relief, "Whew, I felt like someone was watching me."

"Yes — I know that feeling!"

As we quickly drove away, he voiced his favorite saying—"Let's get the hell out of Dodge!"

The local morning news told about the old Hillery home burning down, and how fortunate it was that no one was living there.

"Yeah," I said to the newscaster (like he could hear me) "At least no flesh and blood person."

They determined the fire was most likely caused by bad wiring since it was such an old house. Thank goodness there was no mention of possible arson. The picture that flashed across the TV screen showed the Sad House had burnt totally to the ground.

I said, "Amen!"

My thoughts were of Sara and Adella. I could easily imagine them driving down the road with smiles of determination on their faces and hopes for a brighter future in their hearts.

Perhaps they were saying, "<u>We</u> <u>did</u> <u>it!</u>"

***** PS *****

No more garage or estate sales for me at least for a long time!—Well, for sure nothing like that fancy red pillow or those <u>Black</u> satin <u>Gloves</u>!

"Don't Kick the Rocks"

D on't kick the rocks? Well that is a rather strange way to start a story, isn't it, but later on you will see the significance of that statement.

Camping can be a great adventure, seeing different places from a different perspective and this is what my tale is about.

My husband, Tommy and I started this tradition when our four children were young and to this day they still love being close to nature, as I do. We started out "roughing it" the tent way—probably like most families. Besides visiting kin people, camping vacations were on the agenda each summer and often in-between. It was always fun to plan where we would go on our next camping trip and this usually started while we were driving back home. My husband and I had talked about going to the Big Bend National Park in Texas for many years, but by the time we got around to it, the children were out on their own. After reading about the park and looking at pictures of the beautiful scenery, we decided it was time to visit there in our newly acquired second-hand camper. As luck would have it, one of his cousins and her husband wanted to go so without a doubt that would be more fun plus it is safer to camp and travel with others. If you have ever done this, you know that all kind of things can happen, with the most common being a flat tire or worse, a blowout.

Enough ground work laid, so I'll get on with the tale that makes this camping trip very different.

I will skip the four hundred or so miles we traveled to get to Big Bend other than saying we visited many interesting things along the way. Our second night was spent just outside the park at a private owned campground because our reservations didn't start until the next day. The first day after "settling in" we all took a short hike around the area armed with our cameras. It was April and probably the most popular time to take pictures of the beautiful varieties of cactus that were sprinkled over and around the mountains. This was before the digital cameras so I was loaded down with extra lenses and film. I mention this mainly because, I decided on my next hike I would only take the bare essentials.

The next day our camping buddies chose to visit the Fort Davis Mountain Observatory while my husband and I would take a two-mile hike. The hike would take us up a path that leads to where two cliffs almost join together. It is called "The Window" and is known for the awesome view you have when looking through the open space. I should mention that this hike was more my idea and to humor me Tommy went along with it. However, later I wished he hadn't been so agreeable.

We figured our separate trips would last about the same length and that evening we would sit around a cozy fire telling about our separate adventures.

At the beginning of the trail was the usual park ranger's sign stating important rules to follow, with some underlined. Those were: <u>stay on the marked paths and be sure you let someone know where you would be hiking.</u> No problem! We always tried to do that. There were other safeguard rules covered and we certainly planned to follow them so no problems were anticipated. Best laid plans—hmm—. Right!

I carefully filled my small backpack with essentials. My canteen of water (he had his own), camera, extra film, four packs of peanut-butter crackers, two apples, ace bandage plus a few band aids and a poncho. Even though it was a sunny day and the hike shouldn't take long, the weather is so unpredictable I usually carry one. Also, since I love to identify birds and plants, I always take one or two small books along. Don't laugh, but one is my trusty Euell Gibbons book on edible plants. With sunscreen, good shoes, hat, and backpack on and my trusty walking stick in hand, we started up the rocky trail.

It was a great feeling to be surrounded by such rugged beauty so we took our time enjoying it. After about thirty minutes from the camp headquarters we heard what sounded like the roar of a mountain lion. We knew there had been sighting but were totally surprised to hear the sound of one. My husband reasoned, "It most likely wasn't that close since sounds could echo through the canyons."

I laughed and said, "Well this isn't like Disney Land where they have fake animals appear or make sounds."

Not to be discouraged we continued trudging up and down the rugged trail <u>carefully staying on the main path</u>.

We exchanged greetings with several groups of hikers, most of them younger and moving along at a faster pace. The biggest percent were heading back toward the campground headquarters, I guess. We had gotten a little later start than planned but there was still plenty of time to go at our leisurely pace. I like to stop and check out plants and lizards and take lots of photos. Since we are from flat land country we also needed to take a breathing break pretty often.

Several times we came to a fork in the path so I would place rocks on top of each other indicating the way we had come from. That is something that I do when on an unfamiliar trail. To some people this may seem silly, but the thought of being lost anywhere is not good, and especially in a place this large. Plus the <u>"lions & tigers, oh my!"</u> In case you haven't seen "The Wizard of Oz," that was a joke.

After an hour or so we reached the top of the mountain where the Window formation is situated. As we came around the last curve we surprised a young couple more interested in making love than the scenery. No big deal—but I recall we were more embarrassed than they were.

After a little friendly conversation they told us to take care and were on their way.

We gazed through the opening called "The Window" and it definitely was a breathtaking view. There was a rather dark bank of clouds on the horizon but we assumed they were miles away. Living in Texas all our life we should have taken that as a warning, since we know how fast the weather can change. All we could think of then was to relax and take in all this beauty.

We rested and casually enjoyed our snacks as we listened to the wind as it made a strange moaning sound. It whistled in and out of the crevices like some spirit watching over it. It was easy to imagine that the American Indians who called this their home would have had many watchful eyes guarding against intruders. The evidence is seen in many places around the park where their pictograph art can be found. In fact I had taken a jeep ride to see some while at the private owned campground the day before.

This would have been a perfect place to live with the many types of animals and plants to eat. Without a doubt, there would have been many battles fought over possession of this area. These were some of the things my husband and I were discussing when we were brought back to the present by a distant rumble of thunder.

We had already planned to walk a little faster going back, and with the weather quickly changing—we had no choice. I remarked about the skies being so clear when we left, one would never guessed the weather could change that fast. Tommy replied, "Well—we know, that's one thing Texas is known for."

We were sorry we hadn't checked for possible showers. It doesn't take brains to know that during a heavy rain or thunderstorm, this would be terrible place to be. I'm thinking, slick mountains and possible flash floods. Sounds horrible! I reminded Tommy that we would be fine if we "stayed calm, cool and collected"—. Famous last words!

About a third of the way back to camp we came to the first fork in the path.

Angrily I exclaimed—"Where is my rock marker?"

It was evident someone had kicked the rocks down as they were scattered around the area that I would have put them. Guess they thought they held no special meaning. I had placed the rocks correctly but had not figured the right or left in my head. After studying the paths, we chose the one that was the widest.

We felt the urgency to walk a little faster as the rumbling of thunder was definitely getting closer. The sheer sides of the ravine and dark clouds were blocking out most of the remaining sunlight and to make matters worse – nothing looked familiar. After walking for about fifteen minutes we had the "sinking feeling" that we were indeed lost. Upon closer observation we discovered where we were walking was a dry creek bed rather than a path. If it rained much this would be a devastating place to be because flash floods can occur so quickly.

My husband's sharp comments were—"We are in deep shit" and a bit nicer one being—"We didn't have any business hiking up here in the first place."

Oh well at this point I couldn't help but agreeing with him one hundred percent.

It stood to reason that all we needed to do was simply turn around and go back till we reached the other path. Right?— Okay, that was the plan.

As we retraced our steps a few drops of rain began falling. We walked as fast as we safely could because to twist an ankle or break a bone would spell double trouble. The rain clouds seemed to explode over us, as did the lightning flashes. A puddle here and there started joining together so we moved up a little higher on the bank. We spread the poncho over our heads for awhile but that was slowing us down, so we decided it would be better to look like a couple of drowned rats and get out of this predicament as quickly as possible. Even though we both had shoes with good traction the rocks were quite slippery so we couldn't go as fast as we would have liked. By this time the stream was definitely getting higher and rushing along much faster. We knew we had to get to higher ground, but was also afraid we would miss seeing the path as it entered into what was now a little river. To our horror, there was a different sound echoing just ahead. — One we had never heard before. The roar and crashing of rocks and trees grew louder. My heart was pounding and I'm sure Tommy's was also.

With urgency in his voice, he said, "Climb up fast!"

He grabbed my hand and we scrambled up and around rocks and bushes as quickly as possible as the approaching torrent grew closer. Another big problem was that the water was rushing down in so many places it was impossible to see the original path we had come down. At this point in time that was the least of our worry. Our main objective now was to get to higher ground and stay put for who knows how long.

Nothing remotely like this had ever happened to us before. You can read or hear about other people's encounters with flash floods, but until you personally try to out run one, the feeling is unfathomable. Trudging around rocks we reached an upper level where the ground was more even. Hopefully this was a people path where we would be more likely to be found or hopefully find our own way out in the daylight.

At that moment the ground seemed to shake.

I cried out, "Oh my Lord, what's happening?"

We cautiously looked below where we had been only minutes before. The sound was unbelievably, but the site below was even more so. Rocks and trees were being pushed along at a great speed and eventually that sound gave way to the rushing river and booming thunder. Tommy and I just stood there shaking in disbelief. We both thanked God for helping us get "out of harm's way."

As mentioned earlier, it was early spring so the evenings were cool at this altitude and being soaking wet, we were really cold.

With chattering teeth, my husband said, "Somehow we need to find shelter from this horrible weather." Miraculously, as in answer to our problem—a bolt of lightning struck nearby and all the surroundings were illuminated briefly. At that moment we noticed an over-hanging rock ledge just a few feet from where we stood. I poked my hiking stick all around in the small cave-like area in case snakes were taking refuge in there. Tommy bravely checked it out first. We estimated it was about six feet wide, almost five feet deep, and close to six feet high. It was a perfect place to stay in emergencies like this. I felt like our guarding angel was working overtime trying to save us from that treacherous riverbed.

This would have been a great time to have a small fire with the dry leaves and small branches that had blown into the back corners. There sure would have been no danger of setting this wet mountain on fire. Forget that idea because neither of us smoked so we had no reason to carry a lighter on a short hike. At least it would be a fairly dry and safe place where we could wait this storm out so we gave thanks for that.

We sat there with our backs to the wall shivering and trying to catch our breath. Huddling there I (maybe he did also) felt like crying but what good would that do. By this time the cousins we came camping with were probably back from their "peaceful" trip and wondering why we weren't there. They probably thought we were just sitting at the Lodge waiting for the rain to slow down.

Tommy said, "When we get back to camp this will be pretty embarrassing to explain what happened to us."

"I know how you feel, honey," I muttered. "Talk about being embarrassed for a silly reason—one time when I tripped and had blood running down my leg. I was more worried about someone seeing me being a 'klutz' than I was being hurt. What dumb thoughts!" We agreed we would be so thankful to get back to the safety and warmth of our camper; we wouldn't care what anyone thought.

Within an hour or two it would officially be nighttime but due to the weather, there was little light left. Tommy shook most of the water off the poncho and wrapped it around us, so with our body heat we were a little more comfortable.

We figured we might as well make the best of this rotten deal, so we ate our peanut butter crackers and washed them down with a little water. I say little because we didn't know just how long we would be stuck out here.

As we sat there thinking about the flash flood that we had barely escaped from, it reminded me of the Frio River where we camped many times. We witnessed that small river turn into a raging force once but the difference was we were warned ahead of time plus set-up on high ground. Some were not so lucky. Each year when we came back the river would look so different and now we know why.

We sat silently just listening to the heavy rain and the deep rumbling of thunder as it rolled through the canyons. No help could be expected in dangerous weather like this. Even if the park ranger and his helpers came looking for us, it would be almost impossible to hear anyone call out.

Night was closing in and we were really tired and upset by the frightening events of this day. We decided to take shifts trying to sleep so I told my husband to go first since he seemed extra tired. As I sat there listening to the driving rain and counting between the lightning flashes it all seemed so unreal.

My thoughts began to wander, "Was this really happening to us or was it just a lucid nightmare? Oh how I wished it were!"

It would be the understatement of the year to say we were simply fortunate to get out of the riverbed just in time and find this warm shelter. I really feel our guarding angel was giving us help—just wish that person who kicked my "rock directions" over, was told not to do it.

"P. S., if you see something like that while hiking, don't kick it over!"

Without realizing it, I drifted off to sleep and slipped into a turbulent "dream state." I have no idea how long I slept but when I awoke it was pitch black as there was no lightening to light up the mountainsides.

Thank goodness the rain had stopped. When it gets daylight, finding our way out of here should be a little easier. At least we had gotten pretty warm in our little cave house so I thanked God for that.

I sat there listening to a couple of owls fussing over their territory and other night sounds that I didn't recognize. You know how it is; crickets, frogs and other critters seem to get louder after a rain.

The next sound made me jump so suddenly, it woke my husband up. Chills ran down my spine and probably his too as we heard the screams of a mountain lion/cougar or whatever you call them. There was another "call" in the opposite direction. We sat motionless and hardly breathing, listening for any approaching sounds. My husband had the walking stick in his hand just in case they were heading our way looking for a midnight snack. We could yell and jump up and down, for whatever that's worth but if they were really hungry that probably wouldn't discourage them. Another unpleasant thought was—all cats have padded paws so they can sneak up on their prey with no sound.

Suddenly we could hear the wonderful sounds of humans in the distance calling—"Hello!"—"Hello!"

Without hesitation, we scrambled out of our little pocket cave, calling out "Here!" "Here!"—This was repeated over and over till we saw the beams of many flashlights.

Wow, how great that sight was!

They were all relieved to find us unhurt and apparently no worse for the wear. Tommy and I apologized several times for any problems we had inveterately caused them.

We decided to save our breath, so my husband told our rescuers, "We can tell you guys about our crappy misadventure when we get back to camp."

"Better yet," I suggested, "We need to get a warm shower, a little rest and tell our story in the morning over a cup of hot coffee."

All agreed!

The next morning several people gathered at the Lodge for breakfast and our story. Needless to say there were many comments, exclamations and shaking heads with, "Oh my gosh," being used the most.

I got some strange looks when I said, "Our hike went bad when I discovered someone had kicked my rock directions over." However— after explaining I think everyone understood my meaning.

We learned many lessons from this frightening experience. If I made a list it would be something like this: have a good map, pay more attention to landmarks, check the weather or just don't take a hike in unfamiliar places. Sorry to say but from that time on my husband chose the last one.

*****

The Trick or Treat Anniversary"

P erhaps I could have chosen a different title such as "The Idea That Backfired" or "The Devious Get Paid Back." Better yet if I had gone along with the usual anniversary outing and enjoyed a movie and meal I wouldn't be writing this at all. But no! With my sweetest coaxing voice, I casually remarked to my husband Tom that I would like to do something different for our anniversary. I asked, "Wouldn't you?"

"Like what?" was his answer. I told him I had read about a small historical town in East Texas and thought it would be a fun place to visit. Incidentally, the article was in an October magazine with a Halloween theme. It dealt mainly with some spooky places where you could get your thrills for this time of the year. These things I conveniently did not mention. I told Tom about some of the old hotels where several famous and some notorious people had spent the night. I skipped over the part about being haunted by some of them. The hotel I wanted to stay in is called The Magnolia. The name is pretty but the building in the picture was not fancy at all. I chose it because it was supposed to be the "spookiest." Guess I was in some weird mood by wanting to go there for our anniversary. Silly me! I had never knowingly stayed in a haunted house, so I thought being near Halloween it would be exciting. Tom wasn't too enthusiastic about the idea and if I had mentioned the real reason I wanted to go there, he would have given it a quick veto. I hurried on to tell him some of the interesting things I had read about the town and it was only a few hours away. I assured him I would handle all plans and even drive.

He humored me by saying, "What the heck, since you're dead set on it I might as well agree; who knows it could be fun."

I began making plans as soon as he went outside to work in the yard.

When I called to reserve room number nineteen, the receptionist asked if I was sure as they had much prettier rooms. Bravely I said that was the one I had read about and wanted to spend the night in it to see if I could "sense" anything. I'm sure she figured me to be another "kook" like one of the many strange people who probably came there with that in mind. Actually, that may be the reason they allow these paranormal articles to be published. I explained how much I enjoy spooky books and movies so I figured this would be "right up my alley." She told me some people leave that room in the middle of the night so, if I changed my mind, I could choose another room when we arrived. Hmm, I wondered what was I was getting us into. Surely the place wouldn't be that scary.

By the time the weekend arrived we were both looking forward to an exciting and at least a different kind of anniversary celebration. A movie and dinner is fine but I was ready for something else.

Tom was in a happy mood and said he would drive if I would be the navigator.

"Great", I replied, "That will give me time to read more about The Magnolia Hotel and things to do around the town."

As I read the history about this once important inland port city, I knew we would have an interesting time if nothing else.

Here are a few brief comments I read to Tom. "Originally this hotel was a warehouse built in the 1850's but it shut down when the inland port became unfit for steamboat travel. After a time, a 'prosperous' Madam bought the building and named it The Sweet Magnolia Hotel. She converted it over to accommodate her 'girls' and their special clientele. After a few years she was forced to sell the hotel due to the nature of her business.

It later became a bank, but succumbed to the depression era. Eventually it became a respectable hotel, The Magnolia." One of the last comments the writer made was, "A twisted but lovely old magnolia tree still stands next to the hotel as a reminder of the original Sweet Magnolia Hotel."

On the way there I did tell my unsuspecting husband a little about the possibility of the hotel being haunted, but since he didn't believe in that kind of stuff, it didn't matter to him. I emphasized the antique stores, an old syrup mill and several other historical things we could visit. Tom's interest perked up since his Grandfather had made sugarcane syrup many years ago. He conceded the rest would probably be okay, just none of that silly ghost stuff!

We pulled into the hotel parking lot and I must say that the outward appearance was a little disappointing. Even though I had seen pictures of it online, it seemed even more "stark." It was a simple, two story red brick building. Other than the old twisted magnolia tree, we could see little beauty from the outside. This should have come as no surprise since originally it had been a warehouse, next a house of "ill-repute" and then a bank. The information I had read said, after the bank it was unoccupied for a long time before becoming the quaint and respectable hotel that it is today.

I was beginning to wonder what I had gotten us into, but entering the lobby I felt a sense of relief. It was beautifully decorated with antique furniture so I assumed room number nineteen would be also. We were busy "scoping" the place out while the receptionist was busy talking with a distinctive looking elderly couple.

My husband whispered in my ear, "Thank goodness the place attracts normal looking folks and not just ghost hunters."

I frowned at him and said, "Hmmm, are you saying I'm not a normal person?"

Before Tom could answer, the receptionist said, "Greetings to the Magnolia Hotel, I'll be with you shortly, just make yourselves at home." We smiled and nodded then walked over to the rack of leaflets displaying local and nearby places of interest to visit. Several caught my eye and you might know, the title of one was, "Strange Happenings Here."

Tom said, "Yep, I knew you couldn't resist that one."

I replied, "That's right! It's almost Halloween, so let's have fun and pretend there are some ghosts here." Little did we know that joke would come back to haunt us.

Even though there were scented candles burning, I could still smell a hint of mustiness in the air. Neither paint nor candles can completely hide the scents of a hundred year old building. Whatever—that's to be expected.

The distinguish couple smiled as they walked by us and she declared, "Antiques, here we come!"

The man shook his head in desperation and said, "Credit card, get ready for the slide." We couldn't keep from laughing at his remark.

As the door closed behind them, the receptionist told us they were the only others, so far staying the night—so if we decided to change rooms it would be fine. I understood what she was implying but Tom had no clue. When I think back about the tricky way I got him to go there, I felt a little guilty. Too late now!

We were given keys and directions to our upstairs room. No porters or elevators here, it was a do it yourself thing. Tom carried our suitcase and I had a bag of snacks and a small cooler that held our special wine. As we trudged up the narrow creaking steps, I was already daydreaming about the many folks who had gone up and down these stairs. From boots to high-top heels to business shoes, all with a lust for life. When I think about it, us "moderns" aren't so different. Whatever, if anything—adventure here we come!

Halfway up the stairs I suddenly stopped, and Tom nearly bumped into me. He warned me in a mocking voice "Next time when you're gonna stop, let me know or we might end up haunting this place too."

In the middle of his laughing I said, "Wow, did you feel that?" By the blank look on his face I knew he hadn't felt the rush of cold air that we had just passed through.

The paranormal explanation for this sort of thing might be that some tragedy had occurred in that area and the person's energy force still lingered there. Please excuse that unprofessional description of a ghost or a restless spirit. For some unknown reason I have always been sensitive, as it is called, to that kind of thing. Whatever—it is quite unnerving or startling to say the least.

The hotel receptionist had told us the board floors were the original ones, but they had added the carpet runner down the middle to cut down on the noise. Nonetheless, there were creaks and squeaks ever so often and that added to the atmosphere of this old building. Antique tables were scattered down the long hall with each holding a lovely old lamp that had been converted to electric. However, they still gave the impression of coal oil lamps with their soft glow that seemed to dance and cast shadows along the way.

I said, "Hey Tom—this is going to be fun, don't you think?"

He replied, "Well—I'll answer that one tomorrow."

When we were about twelve feet from our room, I felt a frigid blast of air that sent chills from the top of my head and down my spine. I jumped and called out, "Yikes—what was THAT?"

"What?" exclaimed Tom.

Holding out my arm I said, "Just look at these "goose-bumps!"

Eyes bugging out, he declared, "How did that happen?"

"I don't know Tom," I said, as I walked past the spot again to see if I would get the same results. "WOW! Whatever it is—it's still there." Sorry to say, my husband never felt a thing, but that's probably good. One of us needs to be level headed.

Upon entering our room, we both commented about the dreary appearance but figured this is how a business man's room of the early 1900's might look. To be fair there were some nice antiques, just not the frilly kind that attracts a lady—except for a lovely old bathtub with lion's feet. I would definitely try that out later.

To humor the "down-to-earth" people who didn't wish to stay up at night hoping to see the wisp of a ghost, there was a television. It was sitting on a high shelf facing the bed.

"Wow!" I said, "What a bed! I think I'll need a ladder to get on it."

Tom 'turned-on' his W. C. Field's voice saying, "Ah my little chickadee, I'll boost you up."

"Thank you kind sir! I'm glad you didn't call me Mortisha." We both had a good laugh and I said, "See we haven't had one glass of wine yet and we're already having fun."

Tom said, "Hang onto that thought while I go downstairs to get some ice for our little cooler—that way when we get back from checking the town out, our wine will be ready to check-out."

"Good idea! I'll get a few things out of the suitcase to make this place look a little homier." Glancing around the room, I half expected to see some ghostly figure watching me as I studied the objects in this rather small room. I had read that almost all of the furnishings in the hotel were brought in from other places, so there could be a mixture of "feelings" within these walls. My thoughts wandered to the massive bed with its fine woodcarving on the headboards—it was by far the best piece of furniture in here. However, without the colorful quilts and frilly pillows it would still look pretty cold. They seemed a little out of place with everything else being so masculine, but what lady would want to spend the night in a room like this without some pretty things to look at. Come to think of it, people do not spend the night in room number nineteen with that in mind. I was starting to get a funny feeling about this room and it wasn't the 'ha ha' kind. Tom opened the door, and I was glad he broke my 'train of thought.'

I told him, "We might need one of those warm quilts tonight, since the old iron radiators may not even work. "Wouldn't you hate to be sleeping here in the 'dead of' winter!"

"Yes Mortisha—your choice of words sounds pretty ominous. Remember, we are here to have a fun anniversary!"

"You are absolutely right, Tom! Let's go check the town out."

I received those tingling cold feelings when I crossed the place in the hall and on the staircase as I had before. Naturally I jumped back with some kind of comment.

My husband just laughed saying, "You have an over-active imagination."

"Hmm, you can't fake goose bumps Mr. Smart Pants," I said.

I must admit it felt good to get outside—like back in the real world. We enjoyed looking in several antique shops, and then took a tour of the old syrup plantation. Incidentally, they still sell their delicious sugarcane syrup.

Our feet needed a rest so we decided we would save some shopping for the next day.

There was a quaint little Italian restaurant next to our hotel where we ordered food to go since we had our anniversary wine in the room. In spite of having our meal on the lamp table, it was fun and the wine was good. I might also add—a little smooching that we wouldn't have done in public.

It was time to get comfortable and just relax, so Tom said, "Ladies first."

I didn't argue as the old fashioned tub was beckoning me, so in no time the swirls of steam mixed with sweet smelling bubble bath had me whistling a happy tune. A big rocking chair enticed my hubby—so that's where he landed.

I laughed saying, "I'll leave the door open just in case a 'spook' gets fresh with me." A small marble table sat conveniently by the tub on which I placed two candles that I had brought from home. I was playing this romantic thing to the 'hilt.' I lit the candles and put my glass of wine within reach. The warm relaxing bubbles welcomed me as sank into them. My eyes took in the not so fancy room and followed the wavering candle glow as it tried to make its way to the tall ceiling. I wondered how a tragic event or otherwise, could linger on, but the article I had read said throughout this building and especially this room, unexplainable things still take place. Later maybe I would walk down the stairs and hallway to see if I could detect any other ghostly things. I laughed at my thoughts; like I'm some sort of expert?

My husband called out from the other room saying, "I smell strong cigar smoke—thought this was a smoke free hotel."

I said, "Yes it is, but the magazine article I read also said one of the ghostly things about this room, was the occasional smell of cigar smoke. Oops—sorry I didn't tell you that earlier, Tom, but you would have just laughed."

With a little anger in his voice, he said, "Well, I'm not amused! I'll check-out the hall and below our windows." He had opened them earlier to let the cool autumn breeze in. He walked over to the window and said, "Maybe someone is standing below smoking... Nope! No one down there!"

Within a few minutes the pungent cigar smell was taking over the pleasant aroma of my bubble bath. I shivered as I had the strange sensation that someone was watching me. A sudden cold blast of air whipped through the room and made the candles flicker out. With near panic in my voice, I called out to my husband, and he was there 'on the double.' I was shivering pretty badly as he helped me out of the tub and quickly put a big towel around me.

"What the heck's going on here?" He shouted, "Let's get out of this room; it feels like a fridge!"

Still dripping a bit, I told him what happened—as best I could.

In a shaky voice I said, "After the bathroom filled up with cigar smoke, I felt like someone was watching me—and then—there was a blast of cold air! My warm bath suddenly felt like a pool of ice water."

His next question was, "How on earth did it get so cold in here with no air conditioner?"

I said, "Tom—<u>not</u> <u>of</u> <u>this</u> <u>earth</u> is the Big Clue."

We wasted no time getting into bed and soon felt warm and secure in each other's arms. That was romance enough for me. Tom went to sleep without much trouble ～ but not me. We had left a small light burning in the bathroom, so I was able to see basic shapes in the semi-darkness, and thank goodness, I saw or smelt nothing unusual.

My head was in a whirl as I thought about the eerie happenings. "It" was a frightening experience, but I was not packing up in the middle of the night like some folks had. I would not give the hotel receptionist or that ghost the satisfaction of adding us to their "scaredy cat" list. It shook us up, but I knew there was nothing physical IT could do to us, at least I didn't see how—unless you had a weak heart. Sleep evaded me for most of the night and, when I did drift off, my dreams were of the nightmarish type. Something woke me up rather suddenly, so it took a moment for my brain to register where I was. Looking about the semi dark room, there were small colorful dots of light dancing around. "Wow! How interesting! This must be some of those 'spirit orbs' I had read about. Sometimes they are said to join together and make a human like shape. Well I didn't want that to happen, so I quickly turned my flashlight on. Thank goodness they disappeared—What next? I know I said I wanted a fun and spooky time, but this was more than I bargained for. Just then there was something else. I sat up in bed and strained my ears trying to make out what the distant sound was.

Tom awoke in time to hear what I was hearing and he whispered, "What is that?" To me it sounded a little like metal spoons clinking together and it was getting closer. Whatever it was, it stopped as quickly as it had started. Thank goodness, because I didn't think we could take much more of this place.

In an apologetic voice, I said, "Tom, I sure got my wish for a different type of anniversary celebration; guess you will never understand what possessed me to decide on this hotel."

"Possessed will do!" he answered.

Morning did not come too soon for us, and in no time we were packed and out the door. As we walked several feet from our room, I hurried past the 'cool spot' and said, "Yeah—I feel you Spook, just stay put if it makes you happy!"

Tom gave me a weird look and declared, "What the heck was that all about—saying your final good-byes?"

"That's right, someone else can do the exorcism."

With a cheerful smile, the hotel clerk said, "I see you survived room nineteen; shall we see you two on your next anniversary?"

A little too quickly, we both said, "No thanks!"

Tom said, "I think the wife will most likely settle for a good meal and movie."

"Sounds like a plan dear." Turning to the hotel receptionist I said, "I wanted to do something different this year and, believe me, the 'mission' was accomplished. It will definitely be a night we will not forget. By the way, it lived up-to the tales I had read—and some. Please add us to your 'brave' list."

"Dang 'spooksville'—if you ask me," declared Tom.

"Oh my! I do hope you folks didn't get too upset. 'They' are harmless and not always active—other than giving guest a case of cold chills.—Hmm, and then there are those who checked out in the middle of the night."

"Maybe their bath-water turned to ice water?" I calmly said. Quickly I added, "Nothing wrong with the hotel' utilities, it was just a ghostly prank."

"Ooh no," she said. "Guess we can't count on a good recommendation from you folks."

My husband gave me an odd look when I said, "Well, I think some of my girlfriends and I might just come back here for the heck of it... However, I'll choose a different room."

With a smile the receptionist said, "That will be good—you ladies can find plenty of fun things to do in our little town."

After checking out, we decided we were in no mood for shopping! The spooky hotel with its weird happenings and lack of sleep almost 'did me in.' Oh course I wouldn't admit it to Tom, because he would really tease me big time.

I glanced in the side mirror as my husband drove us home. Silly me, I half expected to see some wispy ghost waving goodbye to us.

I said to my husband, "Listen-up, while I read this unnerving tale to you, it's from one of the brochures I picked up from the hotel." It says, "The sheriff was called often to break-up fights or stop an irate 'customer' from bulling the ladies around. One such night, as he headed down the hall toward room nineteen to rescue a damsel in distress, he was shot. He died within a few feet of the door. To this day some people report sudden cold chills in that area. Often in the 'dead of night' the clink, clink of his spurs can still be heard coming down the hall."

We gave each other a quick look and silently contemplated what we had witnessed.

*****

"The Secret Closet"

Have you ever seen a closet within a closet?
If someone asked me that question, I would probably
answer: "Who would want a closet inside of a closet?
You could store just as much in one larger area."
Actually, this is a story about a secret closet that
was not used for storage at all. It was well hidden
for a terrible reason and my sisters, Nora, Jana and I
discovered the frightening truth.
This happened many years ago when we just children,
but the thoughts of it are forever etched in our
mind—. So now to my spooky closet tale!

We lived in a small northwestern, Texas town; in fact most of our kin people lived near that area. One of our favorite aunts and uncles lived just outside of town in a beautiful old house. They said it was built in the early 1900's and they had owned it since the late 1930's. It had the high ceilings and big rooms, and when we were youngsters they seemed even larger. Everything always looked so special just like our Uncle Alonzo and Aunt Lola. They had lots of pretty furniture and things to admire and always yummy sugar cookies.

Everyone in town referred to them as Aunt Lola and Uncle Alonzo, I guess that was because they were such friendly folks.

They always seemed happy to have us girls visiting, even when our parents weren't along, however, there were a few rules we had to abide by. In my memories, I can still hear Aunt Lola say, "You little wild Indians better go bye bye for now or I'll have your Uncle Alonzo tie you to the bed post!" This brought a laugh from all of us and it also made us behave better. As you can imagine we had many great times playing there until that one awful night. Awful is too mild of a word for it, but that will do for now.

One of our favorite games to play was 'hide and go seek.' It doesn't take much imagination to know there would be lots of places to hide. You know, under those tall beds, behind doors, laundry bins, under a pile of quilts and you may have noticed I didn't mention getting in the closets. Good reason! Aunt Lola told us several times to stay out of the closets especially the one in the corner bedroom. In fact she added, "We keep that door closed for a good reason, so play somewhere else."

Since it was always closed we had no reason to go down that hall. Period! Had never are the key words at this point in time! Knowing us 'nosey' girls she most likely figured we would move things around or wrinkle up the clothes. Aunt Lola knew we had lots of fun trying on old-fashioned clothes so maybe she just didn't want us trying on the ones in that room. Whatever, we wondered, why she had given us such a serious warning about that room and closet. You know the old cliché, 'curiosity killed the cat?' Well what happened wasn't quite that bad, but almost!

One day as we sat around their kitchen table enjoying sugar cookies and milk Uncle Alonzo joined us. We begged him to tell us a story. He had lived a life full of adventure and was proud to pass the tales on. Uncle had just finished one of his funny stories when a serious look came over his face. Aunt Lola said, "What is the world is wrong with you Alonzo?" He said, "Nothing—I guess—I was just thinking about that little child crying." "What child are you talking about?" I asked. With a firm voice, Aunt Lola quickly stated, "Alonzo, forget that, it can't be anything!" He stammered, "I...I know we never saw a child, but—it's been so many years and—." She didn't let him finish just told us it was nothing just their imagination playing tricks on them. Aunt Lola changed the subject. We just stared at each other but our imaginations were already 'running wild.'

The ringing of their phone startled us back to reality. They still had the old time wall phone with an up-to date one sitting on the table below it. Aunt Lola often said she wished the old one still worked. At times she would let us play like it still did and we would take turns being the operator. She would laugh and say, "Now don't answer unless you get the right ring and don't listen in on someone else's call." She would then confess she sometimes did that, by accident of course. Yeah right!

Aunt Lola came back from the phone and said, "Alonzo we need to go out to the Bradley's place, Grace may need us to stay the night. She thinks her husband has had a heart attack." "Oh Lord no!" he stated, "Can you kids stay here and look after the place?" We quickly answered yes. Aunt Lola said, "I'll call your folks to see what they say." She returned saying, "Your mom and dad knew you girls would be happy to stay, and maybe help with some chores." Our uncle said he would appreciate us gathering the eggs in awhile. The snakes and coons were always trying to steal them. We didn't have chickens so we thought that was a fun thing to do. Jana even liked to wash and dry them. Nora and I didn't fuss over that job.

Aunt Lola gathered up a few of things and said, "I'm sure you children will be just fine. There's fried chicken and other things in the refrigerator to eat and plenty of books to occupy your minds with." Uncle Alonzo smiled and winked his eye and said, "I'm sure that is just what you kids plan to do!" There had never been a problem in our town, but he told us to lock the doors after we tended to the chickens. Aunt Lola gave us each a quick kiss and Uncle waved as they walked to their black shiny 1939 Ford. One would never know it was several years old because Uncle Alonzo loved to keep it clean and polished. If a chicken tried to get on it he would threaten it and if that didn't work, it would end up on the dinner table.

As soon as they left we decided to gather the eggs and get them cleaned up. With that little job finished we sat down, finished our milk and cookies and then stared at each other for a few minutes. Almost at the same time we spoke, "Let's go look in that corner bedroom and see if we can hear any crying sounds." We bravely walked down the long hallway to the corner room. Actually I did not feel that brave. Perhaps Nora and Jana felt the same because we grabbed hands about the same time. This would be the chance to really check things out, so we had to take advantage of it. Why? Well kids don't always have logical reasons like adults do—. Yeah—right!

Without our aunt and uncle there, 'things' just didn't feel the same. The house appeared extra quite and larger. What would they think if they saw their inquisitive nieces now?

The door was closed as usual. We never knew why, but we planned to find out. Opening the door slightly we looked around and seeing nothing unusual, we walked in. At the same time we each said, "Phew eee!" The musty smell hung heavy in the air, or lack air. I reminded my sisters it was because the room was always shut up. We saw some kid stuff in this room, so it must have belonged to the people who lived here before because our aunt and uncle didn't have children. Even though Aunt Lola and Uncle Alonzo never had any children of their own, all the kids loved them and vice-versa.

That explained, I will tell you what my fourteen year-old brain thought about the room. It looked like a kid's room but in a 'stiff' sort of way. There were two big size beds with a Teddy bear placed directly in the center of the pillows of each bed. One had a frilly bonnet with only one leg and the other just plain brown with a missing ear. There were also a few toys on a shelf, which were probably put there by an adult since it would have been a high reach for a little kid.... Maybe they had a stool. Neatly placed on the shelf were several wooden toys and three dolls. The first in line was a girl doll with pretty blond curls, but was spoiled by a missing eye. Next there was a baby doll with a torn gown and last, a sad faced boy doll with a missing arm.

Jana sighed, "Poor things! Some kid sure was rough with the toys. Wonder if they got a spanking?"

Thinking back in time the only boy doll I had ever seen was a Charlie McCarthy dummy. Handsome Ken had not been invented yet. Without a doubt these were very old.

"Hey," Nora said, "Why don't we play with them for awhile? We can be careful and not mess-up anything in here. Surely that would be okay."

"Fine with me," I said, "This lonesome old bedroom needs to see some fun."

Jana asked why I called the room lonesome, so I replied, "Wouldn't you be if you were shut-up all time with no faces to see you?"

We had not been in the room long when we heard a sound coming from the direction of the closet.

"Shhh," our youngest sister Jana whispered, "Was that a voice?" We listened intently and decided it was probably just the wind finding its way through a crack in the window.

The ringing of the phone down the hall made us jump! I ran to answer it while my two sisters put the dolls and other toys back on the shelf. They closed the door as they left the room. I mention this because later it was open.

Aunt Lola asked how we were doing and apologized for asking us to watch the house for them. She continued by saying, she had checked with our parents and our mother assured her that we girls would not be afraid to spend the night since that was our favorite place to be anyway. I told her she was right and not to worry because we were having fun. She added, "Mr. Bradley had suffered a mild heart attack and would need to stay in the hospital a day or two for test. His wife, Grace needed them to spend the night with her at her home because she didn't drive." Aunt Lola promised me they would be back home by ten in the morning. Oh yes, the last thing she told me was we could sleep wherever we liked, except their bed of course. I told my sisters everything Aunt Lola had said to me. We jumped for joy at the thought of having a slumber party with no adults around. As you know, no one slumbers at a slumber party. That idea came back to haunt us before the night was over.

Nora, Jana and I went back into the kitchen and helped ourselves to the fried chicken and potato salad. Aunt Lola was sure a good cook! After cleaning up our dishes we asked each other, "Now what?" My middle sister Nora pointed at the magazines on the lamp table and said, "Well, we could look at those." At the same time we each said, "Heck no! "How about 'hide and seek' with no off-limits?" exclaimed Nora.

Jana, said, "You mean we can hide anywhere in the house?"

I guess because I was the oldest, and the bossiest I answered, that's right, just don't mess-up anything or Aunt Lola will get on us." I told them I would let them get the best places first so I sat at the kitchen table with my head down and eyes closed. Counting slowly at first then I got faster on my way to one hundred. We all did that trick.

I remembered the usual places but since this time WE decided it was okay to hide in the closets also, so that is where I mainly looked. Sure enough I soon found Nora hiding under some quilts in our aunt and uncle's closet. She glared at me saying something like, "Don't worry I'll stack them back like they were."

For any of you unfortunate people who never played this kid game, the rule is she would be the next person to count and hunt. Now back to the hunt. I went to the next room calling out "Come out, come out where ever you are. I hear you breathing!" Guess that was said to fool the one hiding, but I don't think it worked too well. As I continued down the hall I saw the corner bedroom door was open. Just as I figured, Jana couldn't resist that room with the toys. I started saying the little verse, "Come out, come out where ever you are, I hear you breathing." First thing in the room I heard a muffled sound a little bit like a kid crying. It didn't sound like her but I figured she was trying to pull one of her jokes on me. When I opened the closet door the foul smell nearly choked me to death. That yucky odor was so strong it must have been trapped there since the first people lived here. I didn't see how Jana could stand to hide in there, but I still heard a rustling sound somewhere inside that closet.

In a demanding voice I said, "Jana, get out of there, it's a bad place to hide. No answer came forth. With my shirttail over my nose, I looked behind all the boxes and things but saw no other place where she could hide. I stormed, "Darn it, where are you?"

From behind me came the puzzled voice of Jana, "I'm here! I heard you in here talking to yourself and I got scared."

I jumped up so fast I bumped my head on the clothes bar.

Nora ran into the room about that time and asked, "What in the world is going on in here?"

Rubbing my head, I practically ran from the room. Breathlessly I said, "I need some fresh air."

Nora was the last one out of the room, so she slammed the bedroom door shut. We wasted no time getting away from that room and to the safe, friendly kitchen.

I told Nora and Jana, "I heard crying sounds coming from the closet and figured it was just Jana playing a trick on me—but she was in back of me."

Jana said, "Bet it's the same little kid crying Uncle Alonzo heard. I wonder why it was so sad."

"Yeah!" I said, "Bet that's why they kept the door closed, to hide those sounds." The big question is—we heard sounds, but no one was there. Around Halloween we liked to joke about ghost, but now thoughts were racing through my head, that there might actually be a real one in that closet.

Thinking back on this, maybe it wasn't too smart of an idea, but "kid like," we were determined to get to the bottom of whatever was in there. In case you have been wondering about our ages; I was fourteen, Nora twelve and Jana seven. That may explain our actions and decisions.

Uncle Alonzo and Aunt Lola had made strawberry ice cream a few days before and told us girls to feel free to eat some, so we figured this was the perfect time. Maybe it would calm us down so we could think this weird thing out. The ice cream was yummy, but did little for our thinking process, as you will see.

For some goofy reason I said, "We could sleep in that room tonight and if it happens again—maybe the three of us can solve the mystery."

So back down the hall we 'fool-hardy' girls went!

I bravely swung the door open and told Nora to help me open the windows so we could get some fresh air in the room. My main concern was that we would get in trouble for being in this room, even though Aunt Lola said we could sleep where we wished. In my heart I knew she wasn't including this one. Nora and I took the musty quilts off the bed and placed them over a cedar chest. It was warm weather so we would only need to use the sheets. Jana wanted to help, so she took her shoes off, climbed up on the tall bed and fluffed the pillows as best she could. Laughing she said, "Hey, this is fun! Glad you thought this up, Betsy."

I went back to the kitchen where I knew our uncle kept some flashlights. He would say, "Now girls, these aren't play toys. Never know when we might get a thunder storm."

Since we were trying to solve a mystery, maybe he wouldn't mind us using them. I turned the hall light on as I returned to the spooky room. Brrrr... I wondered if we really should do this. Well too late now, I wasn't gonna chicken out.

We got in the same bed, with Jana in the middle. It was comfortable enough, and we sure didn't plan to go to sleep. Lots of giggling and talk took place, but mostly just listening. I kept saying, "Don't go to sleep!" After an hour of so we ran out of things to talk about. There were plenty of sounds like crickets, tree frogs, and a creaking board now and then but No kid crying.

I drifted off to sleep even though I tried hard not to. I'm sure Nora and Jana had the same problem. In the middle of the night Nora and I were jarred awake by a chilling cry. It was the hysterical crying of a child! "It's Jana!" I cried.

She had been between us and now she was gone. We grabbed our flashlights and then turned the ceiling light on. Nora and I called out loudly, "Jana! Jana where are you?"

We heard the muffled voice of our sweet Jana, "Help me! Help me!" We hurried to the closet where the calls seemed to be coming from. I pulled the long light cord but nothing happened. By this time we could hear Jana sobbing out of control. Nora and I both were saying everything we could think of to calm her fears, but it was as if she couldn't hear us. The beams of our flashlights took in every part of the closet—but she was not there. "Jana, where are you?" we hollered at the top of our voices. There was a soft sounding knock coming from the panels in back of the clothes. Nora and I pushed the clothes out of the way and began knocking all along the backside. We discovered a small door about three feet tall with a latch on it. I unlocked it and outburst Jana! Our sweet little Jana was sobbing and trembling so hard she could hardly stand, so I scooped her up in my arms. Nora grabbed a flashlight so she could check out the secret closet that Jana had been trapped in. I nearly 'jumped out of my skin' when she let out the most 'blood curdling' screams I've ever heard.

"Oh my God, there's a skeleton in this little closet!" she said in shaky voice. We ran from the room as fast as our legs would carry us. Thank

goodness the hall light was still on, especially since the rest of the house was pitch black.

Nora kept repeating, "A skeleton! A skeleton!"

I fussed at her, "For gosh sakes Nora stop saying that, your scaring Jana even more." Truthfully that was doubtful.

We switched on every light as we made our way to the living room. That was our 'safe place', and also at the opposite end of the house from that haunted closet within a closet. 'Safe place' was the name we had given that room because of the warm and protected feeling we got sitting on the big soft couch with the pillows all around us. Lord knows we needed that after the big scare we had just had.

Nora and I both had our arms around Jana and after thirty minutes or so she calmed down enough to begin her frightening tale.

Between sobs Jana told us, "You all were sleeping when something woke me up; it felt like a finger on my head. That's when I heard crying coming from the closet. I was real quite so y'all wouldn't wake up. I wanted to surprise you by finding the little kid first. I got a flashlight and tiptoed to the closet then opened it all the way. The door squeaked a little but it didn't wake y'all up. It was kinda spooky fun at first—till I smelled that stinky air in the closet. I kept saying—I'm Brave! I'm Brave!

There was knocking in the back of the closet, so I whispered, I'm coming to find you. Why are you hiding in there? There wasn't any answer just a little crying sound. I shined the light up and down and saw a latch like on our screen door. When I opened the little closet door—some—something pulled me inside!"

Jana began sobbing so hard and trembling so badly, we were afraid she was hurt. Nora and I assured her the best we could, that she was safe now and there was no way we would let anything or anybody harm her.

Jana took a deep breath and continued, "There was a Halloween skeleton with torn blue clothes on. Oh—Nooo—Its bony hand looked like it was trying to grab me. I hit it with my flashlight and started banging on the wall. Funny wall—it was covered with a quilt!"

We sat there in a shocked state for awhile then I said, "As soon as it's morning I'm going to take a better look into that spooky closet.

Nora said she would go with me so we could look-out for each other.

"Okay," I said, first we need to put the room back like it was, and then look in that secret closet." Not that we wanted to—but we knew we had to tell our aunt and uncle what we had done—and what we had discovered. In fact; we were not sure what was in that secret closet, except it was too scary. There were too many unanswered questions, like the Halloween skeleton grabbing at Jana and the crying and knocking. Hopefully we would get some answers in the morning.

Curled up next to each other on the sofa, we managed to get a little sleep. It was barely daylight when the roosters told us it was time to get up. We went into the kitchen to have cereal and juice, but had little appetite. Just thinking about what we had to do before and after Aunt Lola and Uncle Alonzo got home, made me shaky.

Jana told us she would stay in the kitchen while we went back to that spooky room.

I gave her a hug and said, "Good, you stay put—maybe look at some of the books—don't worry we will be just fine."

As bravely as possible, Nora and I walked down the hall to the corner bedroom.

"Strange!" I declared, "We did NOT shut this door—but it's closed...." We opened it and entered cautiously.

It took us about thirty minutes to get the room back in order. Now to the worst part—that spooky closet! We had brought flashlights because we remembered the closet light didn't work and the secret room would be extra dark.

Nora said, "You look in while I hold the door open. Don't wanna get trapped like Jana."

"I'm not about to GO inside—just going to poke my head in part ways so I can get a good look." Under my breath I thought—probably a BAD look.

The smell was so strong, I asked Nora to look in the dresser drawer to find a kerchief or something. She returned shortly and handed me a red bandana. Now I was ready to check that spooky closet out—I thought!

As the beam of my flashlight pierced the darkness, I screeched out, "Oh dear God—<u>what</u> <u>is</u> <u>this?</u>" There was a small crumpled up skeleton in old blue clothes. It did <u>not</u> look like a Halloween toy.

Nora said, "See—I told you!"

All inside was covered with a quilt. I quickly glanced around and saw lots of torn-up paper and some pans. That was all I could stand of that gruesome closet so we backed out fast. We shut the main closet door, turned out the light and shut the bedroom door. We hurried back to the sunny kitchen. We told Jana it looked like a real skeleton and thought she was mighty brave to have gone through what she did.

We waited for our aunt and uncle trying to figure out how to begin telling all the crazy things we had done—and what we had found.

When I heard them drive up, my heart was pounding so hard, I thought I would die.

One look at us they knew something was wrong, especially when I said we had something terribly to tell them. They both sat down at the kitchen table with us. From start to finish we took turns with our spooky story, and at times almost crying more because of our frightening experience than for our disobedience to them.

Aunt Lola and Uncle Alonzo looked very serious as he gripped her hand. He spoke in a shaky voice, "See Lola, I knew something was wrong about that room with all its strange sounds. You poor girls must have been scared to death." He was right and we still were.

Aunt Lola sighed, "Alonzo I'm so sorry I made light of those crying sounds I just thought our imagination was pulling tricks on us. What shall we do now?"

"Not that I doubt you girls, but I better take 'a look see' just in case it's not just a toy," replied Uncle Alonzo. He marched down the hall with a flashlight and was back in two flashes. His face was pale and his voice shaking as he said, "My Lord I'm afraid it may be a real skeleton. I'll call the sheriff to come check out what we found in that secret closet. One more thing girls, I heard you say you closed all the doors, well—they were all open."

Aunt Lola gave us each a warm hug told us she forgave us and said, "For once you little wild Indians outdid yourselves."

She put on the big coffeepot and said, "Something tells me we better get ready for a lot of serious talking and questions before the Sheriff starts 'digging' around."

With a little kiss on her cheek our uncle agreed, "Don't worry honey things will be alright."

The Sheriff and his deputy wasted no time getting there. Whatever Uncle Alonzo told them, it got their attention.

The Sheriff and deputy listened to our tale as they drank coffee. He then told us to stay with Aunt Lola while our uncle showed them the way to the possible crime scene. Creepers, we had not thought about that possibility.

After almost an hour, they came back to the kitchen. The serious looks on their faces told it all.

"It's the remains of a child—most likely a boy judging from the clothes. We didn't touch it," replied the Sheriff. He called the coroner and told him to get here ASAP.

Before he began he suggested it would be best if Jana went outside and played in the yard, so she did. They sat down and took notes as they asked us all kind of questions.

Aunt Lola told the Sheriff the people they bought the place from had no children and had stayed there less than a year.

The deputy said, "I recall hearing this place had passed through a lot of hands before you folks bought it. No doubt you two have stayed the longest. People have puzzled over the possible reasons, since it seemed like a peaceful country place."

"Back to the matter at hand—this is basically what we found," said the Sheriff. "I'll tell you 'right up front' this is the most grizzly crime scenes I have ever seen. That poor little soul must have been put in there as a means of punishment. We measured, and that little closet is just a barely over four feet high, so the child most likely couldn't even stand-up. A quilt was tacked on three sides and top to make it almost sound proof, and on the fourth wall, there was oilcloth with printing on it."

His deputy took out a pad and read what it said, "<u>I will not lie!</u> <u>I will not break the toys!</u> <u>I will eat all my food!</u> <u>I will not throw rocks</u>

at the house and chickens! And <u>I will not make my sister cry</u>! In larger letters it read; YOU WILL NOT GET OUT UNTILL YOU MIND!"

The Sheriff cleared his throat and continued, "There were pans—we figured for food and water—and then there was a 'slop-jar.' We discovered another small opening just above the larger door—probably where they put the pans through."

There was not a dry eye in the room. That poor, poor little child! I felt sick to my stomach and I'm sure everyone else did.

Aunt Lola looked at our uncle and cried, "Oh Lord—this is so horrible, that little ghostly soul has been trying to tell people where he died for such a long time."

We all agreed that had to be true as strange as it may sound. All evidence pointed to the paranormal, but needless to say most folks never want to consider that.

I looked out as a vehicle pulled up—it was the hearse from the funeral parlor. It was Mr. Dan, the coroner and another fellow.

After the greetings and handshakes Mr. Dan blared out, "What the heck is going on here?"

The Sheriff replied, "Dan you will see soon enough, IT"S more like a hell-of-a-thing that actually took place here a long, long time ago. If it's the last thing I do on this earth before I die, I'll get those devilish parents who did this!"

I recall the surprised look on Mr. Dan's and his helper's faces as they followed the Sheriff down the hall.

He said, "Lord Sheriff—I've never seen you so upset!"

Uncle Alonzo and Aunt Lola gave Nora and me a warm hug and told us they thought it would be best if we went home now. Our folks were probably wondering why we were staying so long. We lived only a mile from our aunt and uncle's house, and that day we walked it extra fast. I was 'busting at the seams' to tell Mom and Dad this spooky story and I knew Nora and Jana felt the same way.

Uncle Alonzo had told the Sheriff we needed rest after all we had been through, besides he knew where we lived if he needed to ask any more questions. His words were still clear as he reminded us, "The law wouldn't want this 'gosh awful' thing to get around now, so tell only your folks and tell them not to pass it on. I'm sure they will understand why."

The next day Aunt Lola drove over to fill us in on further details that were going on at their house. She confided, "Alonzo needed to stay around there to watch out for their things. After you girls left one of the fellows took a chainsaw and had to cut the backside of the closet out so they could get the little boys remains out. Sooo terrible ⁓ and to think, IT was in our house all these years. We sensed a reason to keep that bedroom door closed, but we never never in our wildest dreams could have guessed anything like this."

Without a doubt we will forever think of that poor helpless little boy dying in that horrible secret closet, which was his padded cell. The person or persons who did this unspeakable thing...They must have made Satan proud.

I will wrap-up this tragic and frightening story by including some highlights from an article that appeared in our weekly newspaper, in fact it was probably in several throughout the nation. I'm including only the sordid information not mentioned in my story.... These things were brought to light after a thorough investigation.

"Examination of the skeleton proved to be that of a boy around the age of seven and test showed he had died approximately sixty years ago. The remains were in fair condition due to the almost airtight room. Besides the three foot main entrance door, which would have been latched most of the time, a second smaller door was found near the outside corner of the small closet. This was probably his only source of air and where food etc. would have been passed through.

The courthouse records listed a man by the name A. K. Jasonneski had bought the property and built a house in 1910. Census was taken two years later listing him, his wife, M. A. and two children, a boy and a girl twins. Apparently they moved away in 1918 because, the property was purchased by another family in 1919."

The article stated, "The property had gone through a number of families, but the present owners have lived there the longest."

In an interview with them the husband, we will call Mr. A., said, "We admit there were some unsettling sounds, but we always reasoned they must have been from natural sources."

Mrs. L. agreed and added, "We were determined to make the best of things, because we loved our home. However, it breaks our hearts to think of all the pain that was hidden there."

Now back to the report. "One of the oldest and sharpest ladies in town recalled her parents talking about the Jasonneski family." This is what she told the reporter, "They were stern faced and unfriendly. They had twins, a boy and girl, but few people ever saw the boy and when they did he looked sick or very sad. One time in town the little girl kicked her brother and when he returned the kick, the father yanked him by the arm and walloped him real hard. My mother said it was useless trying to be friendly or visit them; they would never invite anyone in. My father said they moved out suddenly without notice to anyone."

A statement made by the Sheriff determined, "There were more than enough facts to officially charge A. K. and M. A. Jasonneski with the grim murder of their small son. Furthermore, in the process of tracing them down, it has been learned, they both died in a home fire many years ago. It seems the Jasonneski's received punishment for their hideous crime on this earth after all."

After reading that Uncle Alonzo said, "It is written, "Vengeance is mine, says the Lord, so I guess they got a 'double dose' of Hell fire."

There were many prayers said for that poor little boy's soul. We hoped he had finally found freedom.

The decision was made that his remains should be cremated and scattered among the beautiful flowering fields near town. No padded casket for him—he had lived and died in one of those hideous things in his young life.

One more thing I must tell you, "Uncle Alonzo and Aunt Lola moved in with us for awhile. They loved their property and most of the house, so they decided they would just get rid of the bad part.

Aunt Lola motto was, "The more good thoughts you have, the more control you have over bad ones."

They hired carpenters to completely remove the corner bedroom with its evil secret closet. The house looked just perfect when they finished.

Aunt Lola said, "Alonzo and I just didn't realize what a terrible burden we had been living under till now. At last the whole house is truly ours!

In closing I will say we all spent many more happy years there.

****

"The Iris Patch"

"The Iris Patch!" Now what could possibly be ghostly about a patch of Iris? I love flowers, and to me the Iris is one of the most beautiful. However, the Iris plants I'm writing about proved to possess much more than simple beauty as if that were not enough. Fact is they seemed to have a mind of their own. Sounds crazy? Yes! Well here is my story.

My husband's parents live on a farm about a hundred miles from our place in the city; in fact this is where he lived until college age.

We visited them often, and my most favorite time was in the springtime when the roadsides and fields were blanketed with beautiful wildflowers. Many times in past trips I had noticed a patch of green blades in a ditch along the country road a few miles from where his parents lived. I recognized them as Iris plants since I have several types in my yard. My husband, Neil, and I reasoned that it had been a home-site many years before because there was also a small pile of red bricks almost hidden by the weeds.

The following spring the patch of Irises was a sight to behold. They looked like a field of snow. Sooo beautiful! I had Neil stop the car so I could take some photos and study them more closely. They were a little different variety than any I had ever seen before. There were delicate pink veins in the throat part traveling almost to the end of the inner pedals. I talked him into digging up a few of the rhizomes, as their roots are called. Even though it wasn't the time of the year to plant them, I could at least enjoy the blooms for awhile.

He scolded me saying, "You are going to get me thrown in jail yet!" I smiled and told him I would bring him some cookies and a bouquet of the Iris.

We asked Neil's folks if they knew who owned the land where the Irises were growing, and they said no. His mother told us she had asked different people and everyone said it had been uninhabited for as long as they could remember. His dad said if we really wanted to know, we should come during the week and perhaps get the answer at the courthouse. That was a good idea, but we didn't pursue it, so guess it really didn't matter.

Whatever, I was glad to finally have some of the plants since I have admired them for several years. I would plant them in my special area.

From the bay window of my kitchen, I can see the most beautiful part of my yard. I call it my sanctuary. We made a little pea-gravel path leading to a bench that sits near a beautiful Mimosa tree and next to it is an angel statue and a lovely rock fountain that Neil had made. Naturally I have soothing wind chimes and everything to attract birds and butterflies. As you can imagine, it is both peaceful and inspiring.

I have many sectioned off areas for my bulb plants, herbs etc. and that is where I planted my new 'country Iris.'

The following morning I walked down the pea-gravel path with a steaming cup of coffee and a towel to dry off my bench. When time permitted, this was my usual routine. Even in the city a person can create a peaceful spot. Heaven knows we need it!

The early morning sun made the dew glisten like little rainbows on the flowers and other plants and I thought to myself—"I wonder if 'they' are making friends with the country Iris?" Silly me! Like plants can think?

I towel dried the bench and sat down to enjoy my coffee. Glancing in the direction of my new Irises I felt sad because they looked so sad drooping their pretty heads over. Guess it was the shock of being transplanted. I got up to examine them more closely and noticed the once pink veins in the throat part were now blood red. Now that was odd! Without thinking I said, "You beautiful Irises, I hope you will feel better soon."

Neighbors can't see me in my little sanctuary—not that it matters—so I often talk to my plants. Sounds weird to say the least but sometimes it seems to work.

I sat down and enjoyed my coffee and the birds singing their good morning songs.

The following week I was unable to enjoy my special place due to several days of heavy rain and a busy schedule. However, from my window I could tell my country Irises were standing up a little taller.

Finally I was able to get back to my routine of morning coffee in my little sanctuary. As I walked down the pea gravel path I whistled "Oh What a Beautiful Morning" and didn't care who heard me.

My plants looked much perkier after the nice rains, especially the new Iris.

As I sat there drinking my coffee I could hear someone else whistling. It sounded like the old fashioned tune my grandma used to hum. Who could it be and where were they? I walked all around the fence and saw no one. Oh well, I figured the person had walked on by—probably one of my neighbor's grandparents visiting.

I didn't have anything special to do that morning so I got more coffee and a book to read and walked back to my bench. The whistling began again. I'm thinking if I whistle along with them, maybe they will show their face. I started and 'they' stopped. Oh well, I tried.

When Neil got home that evening I told him about the mysterious whistler.

He laughed and said, "Guess you have a secret admirer."

Off and on over the next few weeks I heard the same old-fashioned tune from the invisible person but, sorry to say, Neil never did.

One month or so later my peaceful little sanctuary became anything but peaceful. I was enjoying my morning coffee and a sweet roll when the strangest feeling came over me.

First there was a slight digging sound and a muted "No—no!" Jumping to my feet I walked to where the sounds seemed to be coming from. No one was in the yard but me so I didn't have a clue where the "No, no" voice came from. I looked at my country Irises and something had dug them up. "Darn! They were looking so pretty." Nothing else was disturbed but them. I knew armadillos would do that but I had never seen them in the city. After I replanted them, I went back inside.

Too many weird things were disturbing my peaceful place and me. Could it possibly have something to do with the Iris? Strange question, but everything was fine until we brought them here.

The next day I checked out my flowerbeds and, to my dismay—the country Irises had been dug up again—. Nothing else!

We received a phone call from Neil's dad that evening saying he had some disturbing news regarding the Iris patch.

He told us, "A road crew had started widening that stretch of road and discovered a wooden coffin under the patch of Irises. They were required to stop their work until proper authorities were notified." He added, "They covered it back up had marked the area with yellow tape."

Since it was Friday Neil and I decided to drive there for the weekend and see firsthand what was taking place.

Saturday morning not long after we got to his folk's house, we all drove to where the mysterious Iris patch saga was unfolding.

Two officially marked vehicles were there; one being the County Sheriff's and the other was marked The Justice of Peace. A couple of fellows with shovels were busy digging around the once beautiful Irises, while a group of serious looking guys were huddled around a partially exposed wooden coffin. We stayed out of their way so they didn't ask us to leave. However—we were near enough to hear most of what they were saying.

When the workers cleared the dirt from the top, one guy shouted out, "Hey—we have a name here!" With a brush he swept off the remaining soil and said, "By jiggers, that was mighty thoughtful of someone to hand carve this information. It says, Mrs. Iris May Johnson, B. 1887, D. 1904, husbun J. K. Johnson."

I thought how fitting to have a beautiful patch of Irises marking the spot for his young wife named Iris. Quick figuring told me she was seventeen when she died. I had heard it was common in 'the olden days' for girls to be married by age fifteen, so perhaps she had even been a mother. How sad to die so young!

We heard the Sheriff say, "Well Mr. J. P. what's the next step here?"

He cleared his throat and said, "First I'll go to the court house to see who owns this land then check the Death Books of that time period. That might give us a clue if there are other bodies buried here. We're lucky our courthouse didn't get burned down like so many Texas towns did. Meanwhile, get some more help out here to check this whole area to see if there are more graves."

The Sheriff commented, "Most likely her husband J. K. Johnson and other family members could be buried nearby."

In an excited voice Neil's Dad exclaimed, "My gosh, that is one of our distant kin people!"

The Sheriff turned in our direction and asked, "Do you folks have some interest in all this?"

In an apologetic voice, Neil's dad said, "The person in that grave was actually a distant relative of mine. I never knew that great-uncle because he died before I was born but I remember his name was listed on a 'family-tree' in an old bible that I have."

"Well how about that for a coincident?" declared the Sheriff.

The Justice of the peace got his address and phone number in case he needed more information and in turn gave them his business card. Neil's dad and mother both asked questions regarding what would become of the grave or graves.

The J. P. said, "He would look for their names in the death record books of the early 1900's then talk to the County Judge regarding the matter. They would find the person or persons who owned the land and inform them about the burial location and other details."

Neil's dad whispered to us, "Let's go back to the car, I want to ask you all something."

When we got away from the others, my mother-in-law said, "I can tell you for sure he has some big plan 'up his sleeve' when he uses that tone of voice."

"You are right as usual, Hon!" he said, "I'm thinking since this Iris person and maybe other ancestors of ours will be needing a more permanent home, they could be reburied at the far end of our property.

It would not be that much trouble to keep the area up, at least better than it was. I'm sure that would all depend on the County Judge and what legal steps would need to be taken."

We all agreed it would be a nice thing to do so we returned back to where the officials were. They had started scouting around for other possible gravesites.

Neil's dad approached the J. P. and told him what he proposed to do if it was legal.

With a surprised look the J. P. smiled and said, "Well Sir that would solve one BIG problem! I'll tell the Judge and get back to you as soon as possible."

I thought this would be a good time for my request so I asked him—"If the Judge granted that—could I also relocate all of the beautiful Irises to that area?"

He replied, "I will definitely try as I'm sure that would make Mrs. Iris Johnson happy."

I smiled and thanked him.

One of the fellows with a shovel muttered, "We made a mess of this bunch uh flowers but guess you kin separate em out."

I asked the Sheriff and Justice of Peace if it would be ok if I came back later that day to work with the Irises.

The sheriff said, "No problem, just watch out for holes as they would be checking around for other possible graves."

I couldn't get over how friendly and understanding these guys were, you would never see that in a large city.

Later on that day all four of us came back to rescue the Iris patch. As we worked men were combing the area for more graves.

Suddenly someone shouted, "There's one over by these here red bricks. Might be another!"

Sure enough, it was the grave of Neil's great uncle, J. K. Johnson. The red bricks had been placed on top of his grave and when they removed them they found a flat marble headstone with his information. The dates listed were, born 1871, died 1922. Next to it they found his second wife's marker. It had fallen face down but it was still legible.

We all secretly hoped that would be all the graves found there—after all they wouldn't want the entire second wife's kin buried on their property. Oh well—I figured the Justice of Peace or Judge would work that out later if needed.

As I was digging up the Iris rhizomes (roots) my shovel struck something hard. It was about five feet from where the young Mrs. Iris' grave was. I called out to the man in charge of the operation and he quickly came to see what I had found.

He carefully dug the dirt away from a small wooden box. Brushing the remaining dirt from the top revealed these words, "Baby Iris—here two days."

I could not help shedding a few tears as I thought about this young mother that died in childbirth and then her baby. What a terrible time that had to be for her husband—yet with loving care he had patiently carved their names on the pine coffins and even planted Irises on their graves.

The fellow put a thin layer of dirt over the small coffin then placed a yellow flag on top of that grave as he had the others. He then strung the yellow warning tape around the area with her mother's.

The official ruling was to have rotating guards at the site until Monday, and then the searching job would resume. If no more graves were found within a fourth of an acre, the hunt would be closed.

The J. P. promised to keep us informed and was sure the County Judge would be happy with our request.

Two weeks later we were heading back to Neil's parents home to watch the re-internment of the four bodies that were found. Earlier that morning Neil's dad had directed the coroner and several men to the area where the new gravesite would be. By the time we arrived the four wooden coffins had been reburied and covered with dirt.

The Justice on Peace and the Judge were present to view the final resting-place of the J. K. Johnson family.

After they delivered some official sounding words I was given the honor of praying for these special folks. I think if they could look down on this, they too would be much happier. I know we all felt better now that this strange ordeal was finished.

After the Judge and J. P. left and Neil's folks walked back to their house.

With our small shovels we began working the Irises into the soft dirt on top of the graves. I was so happy to see some of the blooms were still in pretty good shape. No one had planted flowers on Mr. Johnson's or his second wife's graves, but at least someone had gone to the expense of placing headstones.

As my husband and I had just finished planting the Irises on top of all the graves, we began hearing a soft humming sound.

Looking at each other we spoke at the same time, "Was that you?" The answers were "NO!" The humming continued and soon an unseen whistler joined it.

I declared, "Oh my gosh , Neil --- that is the same tune I heard in our back yard. You remember I told you a person was whistling but I never saw them. Good reason since it was a ghost!"

I had never seen Neil so pale as he exclaimed, "My Lord, what a weird thing!"

It was more startling in a creepy way than frightening. The muted happy tune lasted only a minute or so and then drifted into blissful silence, other than the singing birds.

"Wow," he breathlessly said, "Let's get our tools and get back to normal surroundings!"

Hand in hand we quietly walked the path to his parent's house. Guess we were 'at a loss for words' but I thought to myself, at least those dear souls sounded perfectly contented.

Neil's parents listened to our 'far out tale' in disbelief.

A few days after that they called to tell us they actually heard for themselves.

"Stranger than fiction," is what his mom declared.

Like I said originally, "I talk to my plants—but I've never had them talk to me." Come to think about it—that's what I would prefer.

Oh yes I must tell you, the throats of my country Irises turned back to their original pink and also about them being uprooted, I don't feel it was just a coincident. It happened at the same time the grave was being uncovered.

Thank goodness everything is once again peaceful in my back-yard sanctuary. Oh yes, so is the little graveyard on my in-laws place. The

Iris Patch with its beauty and memories will always be one of my favorite places to visit, especially in the springtime.

Perhaps you will think of this as you travel down a country road and see an Iris patch in the middle of a field or in a ditch. Who knows what else is there!

*****

"The Bridge of Terror"

Every time I see skid marks near a bridge that stop at a damaged guardrail, it reminds me of a spine-chilling thing that happened to me. Yesterday, as I noticed heavy black tire marks ending directly against a twisted guardrail, I decided it was time I wrote about my encounter with a "bridge of terror."

Please forgive me if I occasionally switch from past to present tense as I feel it may explain the situation better.

First off I should tell you a little about myself. I know if a stranger walked up to me with a 'yarn' remotely like the one I'm going to tell you, I couldn't back away from them fast enough... Before this happened, everyone who knows me would testify that I'm not the kind of guy to fall for spooky or supernatural tales. Fact is I would have fallen into the skeptical category. Key word here is—would have!

Actually, the weirdest thing about me is, sometimes I'm a traveling salesman. In times like today that is almost unheard of, however, a few of my customers still like it that way.

I consider myself a normal looking guy—maybe a couple of numbers less than Keanu Reeves. I laugh as I say that because a girl I once dated told me that. As I recall, that was probably the best compliment I had from her. Another thing—if I didn't run and bike ride when I got the chance, I would definitely find myself hanging over the café and plane seats that I frequent regularly.

Before getting into my strange tale, here's just a little about my line of work. Our company sells a wide variety of home accessories to both large and small businesses. My dad and uncle started the joint concern two years after I was born. My mom passed away shortly after my high school days and Dad just a few years ago. I couldn't have had better mentors or caring parents. They had an agreement, that at age thirty-three, I would be an equal partner with whoever remained. Incidentally, that will be in just two years. My uncle and I have some good laughs about that because he already calls me Little Boss as I have helped in the warehouse since age sixteen.

Now that that's out of the way, I'll get on with my frightening story. By the way, my name is Allen Franklin.

The incidents I'm writing about happened a little over three years ago, but I recall each detail as if it were yesterday. I will always be puzzled that such a thing could possibly occur—but it did, and it opened my eyes to a "dark side" that exists. As I think back on what started out as a normal business trip, I shutter at how quickly things can change. My travels take me all over the state of Texas whether by plane or car, so I've seen fatal accidents and had some near misses. Nothing shook me up like the events of that day.

Naturally the largest portion of our orders are handled over the phone and internet, but as I said earlier, some customers still like to talk with a person face to face. Well, this was one of those times where I had business in two adjacent towns. It involved a little extra driving and time, but occasionally I didn't mind and in fact, the change was good. If time isn't the main factor, I actually enjoy the rural scenery to the mad dash of the freeways.

When going to a new place I would use the map planner on my computer and sometimes drag out the old fashioned map. However, since my encounter with the 'bridge of terror'— I now own a GPS. Come to think about it—I may have been directed to that route anyway. Never know! Whatever—my normal day to a normal town ended up in Spooksville.

That particular day I flew into Houston's Bush Intercontinental. I picked up a rent car and headed North on I-45. It was a great day to be traveling, which was good since part of this route was entirely new to me. After an hour or so I came to my exit with no problem and immediately found myself on 'the right path.' I say path because it was a two-lane road full of curves and fair size hills, so I had to adjust my thinking and speed right away. As luck would have it, I found myself in back of a very dilapidated pick-up truck that could hardly make it up the hills. I told myself to chill out, I'd have plenty of time to visit both stores and get back to Houston by night. If some unforeseen delay occurred, I could find a motel in one of the little towns and relax since it was Friday. It would be no big deal, because I had nothing pressing till Tuesday. A call to my uncle would be it—no one else was expecting me. A peaceful weekend away from the big city would do me good. No meetings till Tuesday morning, so I could be a little flexible. Flexible! That was the key wording my dad used a lot.

Back to the present problem of trying to be semi-patient as I unwillingly followed this old pick-up-truck that never hit over fifty miles an hour. The few times when there was a spot to pass there was oncoming traffic, so I had to hang back. By now there was quite a parade of aggravated drivers in back of me, so I hoped no one would pull a dumb move and cause a wreck... I reminded myself again to keep cool and enjoy the scenery.

Rebuking myself, I said aloud, "Well, Allen, you said you enjoyed driving country roads. So here you are!" With that said, I studied the landscape a little better. Well it was peaceful—mostly hay fields. Food for cattle no doubt, but the most I know about beef is how I like it cooked.

As we trailed along at a snail's pace, I tried getting my mind off this slow roller in front by thinking about meeting the new clients. We could always use more prospective buyers. The diversion worked for awhile—but not long enough.

You know how it is—after awhile you start wondering what this person leading the pack is thinking—if anything! Could be that guy is getting a "kick" out of delaying all of us—or—maybe he's doing the best he can. Good thought, at least it cooled me down for awhile.

The person in the old truck signaled to turn and that's when I saw he was probably pushing ninety. I felt rotten for my impatience. After he turned off, most of the drivers in back of me went nuts trying to make up for lost time.

The rest of my drive to the first stop was non-irritating—just way past my lunchtime. I was hungry as one of those proverbial bears that I hope never to meet. Lunch would have to wait till after my first meeting. I just hoped my belly wouldn't start rumbling like a Harley. A glance at the clock told me I wouldn't be late for my appointment. Thank goodness for that. Even though it was a fair size town, the store was on the main highway so I had no problem finding it. The owner of the furniture store met me at the door with a big smile and handshake. Best of all she placed a nice order, which certainly made the trip worthwhile. Before leaving I asked her if there was a good place to eat nearby.

She said, "There's a small café on the square that serves a super good 'blue plate' special. If you eat the whole thing, believe me you will be stuffed when you leave." I thanked her and found the café on the square. Against my better judgment, I ate the special plus a piece of their apple pie. I enjoy eating in a place like this—but—there's the hanging over the seat deal. I needed to work this meal off, but I would be behind the wheel for about twenty more miles. While I ate I studied the road map, comparing it to the one I had printed off the PC. Main thing, I didn't want to get lost or slowed down by more 'laid-back' drivers. On closer inspection, I noticed another road that appeared to be the same type I had been traveling on, and it was several miles closer. As I was leaving, I asked the waitress if she knew of any roadwork that direction.

She told me, "Not to my knowledge—. How'd you like the food?"

My answer was, "Great except I just added five more pounds."

She laughed and said, "No way! I could tell right away, you're one of those 'city slickers' that pump iron."

I gave a bigger laugh—and a bigger tip.

After topping off my gas tank at the pump, I made the decision to go the different route... Big mistake!

The road was no worse than the one I had just traveled on, and there was little traffic. For awhile I enjoyed looking at the scenery that had turned into timber country. Tall pine trees lined the highway and as the sun flickered between them, it started doing a 'number' on my eyes. In fact, I felt as though I was being hypnotized. Never have been, but this could be what it feels like.

I seldom get drowsy while driving, but suddenly my eyes became hard to focus. No coffee shop out here! No shoulder to pull off on where

I could at least walk around the car a few times to wake up. I noticed a little dirt road up ahead, but there was a barrier of rocks and a sign saying 'Closed.' I rolled the window down to get some fresh air and turned the music up louder. This worked for a short while, but then I started nodding off again. I shook my head trying to 'clear the cobwebs' out of my brain... Didn't work!

I reasoned with myself saying, "It must be from that big meal I ate—never happened before—Lord—hope I'm not getting sick!"

Thank goodness my eyes cleared enough to see a logging road ahead. I pulled partly into it and got out. Breathing deeply I stretched my legs for a few minutes. I had only made a couple of trips around my car when I saw a big truck heading down the one lane road toward me. Needless to say, I lost no time backing out of there. So, back on the road again, this time I had a logging truck in back of me.

To my aggravation I immediately felt very sleepy—even worse than before.

I cried out, "What the hell is the matter with me—? Get focused!" I knew if this feeling didn't pass before I got to my next stop, they would think I was on some kind of drugs... Surely the town isn't much farther away—I kept telling myself.

Looking in my rear view mirror, I noticed the logging truck was no longer in back of me! I recall thinking, where in the heck did it go—? I hadn't seen any side roads, but in my weird condition—who knows?

In its place, there was an eighteen-wheeler. The driver was keeping some distance back, guess I was driving pretty erratic. In a daze, I recalled I had always prided myself for being a good driver—but right then, I didn't even feel like myself. Straining my eyes, I got a glimpse of a sign saying it was seven miles to Mills, which is where my meeting was. I looked at the time and it was only 3:45 in the afternoon—so I had plenty of time for my appointment—if I could clear my head. I've seen re-runs of the old "Twilight Zone" TV show—and right then, I felt like the main character in one of those.

Briefly my mind cleared enough to think about what I needed to do. My appointment was scheduled for around 4:30 so I would have time to tank up on some strong coffee and maybe take a short snooze before my meeting. I would take some extra coffee on the trip back to Houston, and definitely stick to the freeways when possible. These plans drifted away as I felt another wave of drowsiness grabbing at me.

—Okay people—as you will see, from here on out I'll be switching from past to present tense regularly in order to give you the full thrust of this spooky tale. Hope it doesn't 'bug' the heck out of any of you grammar pros. I think you may understand my story better as I try to explain the many unexplainable things that revolved around that bridge of terror—my bridge of terror.

I heard myself say, "Thoughts—harder—to form... Losing control."

I had the strong urge to pull off the road even though there was no place to safely do that. Between nodding off I noticed the truck was still in back of me—but not too close.

I shook my head violently and turned the radio louder—but nothing helped!

Suddenly there was a frigid blast of air that chilled me to the bone! That woke me up with a start and I shouted out, "What the hell was that?" It was so cold in the car; it almost took my breath away. Either I was going nuts or in a lucid nightmare... Whatever was going on, it was trying to get the best of me and almost succeeding. If that wasn't enough I started hearing an odd sound like a low moan. I switched the radio off so I could hear better... I had never heard a sound like that coming from a car—but what could it be? In the midst of this I noticed a sign with the name of a river on it which meant I would be coming to a bridge soon. I figured there would be a place to pull over where I could see what the devil was going on with my car—and me. The chill and sounds suddenly got more intense and to top that off—the steering wheel was not responding to me... It felt like someone's hands were on top of mine—trying to steer me go off the road... Hands of ice! To my horror I could see a bridge not far ahead—and that was the direction this unseen force was taking me. I gripped the wheel so hard it seemed my hands would break.

The moaning now sounded like a distant—"Help me," over—and over.

Between fighting the wheel and hearing those unearthly cries for help—I was carefully applying my brakes. "This thing" seemed intent on running me off the bridge.

I'm like a lot of people about waiting until serious trouble comes along to ask God for help... "Right?"—Well now was the time—Big-Time!

The burnt tire marks my car was following seemed to indicate another poor soul had encountered the same suicidal demon that I had. "It" was trying to control my car and doing a darn good job of it. The car seemed to vibrate with the cold air, as the cries for help became more desperate—and I sped closer to the bridge.

Suddenly a loud blast from a horn snapped me out of a near trance—and almost certain death. It was an eighteen-wheeler, probably the one that had been following behind me earlier. The driver had closed the space between us as I fought for my life... Thank God for his warning.

My heart felt like it was about to pound out of my chest as I fought to avoid the bridge. Everything seemed to be in slow motion as the screeching of my brakes drowned out all other sounds... Then silence—! The car had finally come to a stop—just inches from the old concrete bridge.

I let out a huge sigh of relief—"Whew—I'm alive!"

I stared blankly at that terrible bridge... It had acted like a magnet—or was it those powerful hands of ice? What about the moans that turned into cries for help—? What or who did they belonged to? Questions—and more questions. Things like this don't happen in the real world, but it just did.

My thinking started improving gradually as I realized the air was warm again. I backed away from the railing, crossed over the bridge, and found a spot to pull off the road. The truck driver parked a little ways in front of me. Running up to my car he said, "Hey fellow, are you okay?"

My voice was shaking as I said—"I—I guess... Honestly—I'm not drunk or a mental case, but it probably looked like it by the way I was driving."

The truck driver said, "I've been in back of you for about fifteen minutes, and first off I figured you must have had a few too many—but then again—I've heard stories about this bridge." Whatever, his sincere voice and face showed he was greatly relieved to see I was unhurt.

I told him, "I owe my life to you and your loud horn"—and almost in a whisper—"And to God."

He said in a strong voice, "Look buddy don't ever be ashamed to thank the good Lord for things, I wouldn't be here today if it weren't for Him."

I gave him a handshake and agreed.

This fellow said, "Follow me into town and I'll treat us to a pot of coffee—and try to think this thing out—by the way my name is Kyle Adams."

In a weak voice I said—"I'm Allen Franklin and I definitely need to figure out what all that crap was about, if possible... Coffee sounds good!"

Kyle Adams patted me on the shoulder and said, "Young fellow, I sort-of understand how you're feeling. Now let's get away from this 'no count' bridge. Folks around here call it 'the bridge of terror'."

He climbed up into his truck and pulled back onto the road, and I followed him like a robot. I had a weird, detached feeling as I wiped the cold sweat off my forehead. At least my mind and body had begun to relax a little at the thought of being in the presence of some real people. That 'bridge of terror' must be harboring some form of sub-human thing... I almost smiled as I thought; maybe it was an ogre.

This Kyle Adams fellow signaled and turned into a parking lot where several eighteen-wheelers and a few cars were parked in front of a neat white building. The sign read, Top Spot Café. Maybe it got its name due to good food or because it sat on a small hill.

Stepping down from his truck Kyle said, "Well—this is it!"

Whatever, I was glad to be here. I gave a sigh of relief as I said, "Mr. Adams it sure is good to get out of the car and into the sunshine." Trying to sound normal I commented, "I've been told to look for the place with the most big rigs and you'll find the best food and coffee in town."

He gave me a serious look and said, "First off Allen, let's not have any more of that Mr. stuff; just call me Kyle. To answer your question, most of the times that's true, but sometimes we get tired or hungry and just stop wherever we can." He continued on with, "Place is clean and the folks are real friendly, so that makes it number one on my list.

You can't beat the hamburgers and onion rings and that's what I'm smelling right now."

As we entered, several people greeted him warmly by name and got up to shake his hand. He introduced me like I was an old friend, and I sure needed that.

The waitress gave Kyle a big hug and said, "Long time no see!" She gave me a smile and said, "Any friend of Kyle's is more than welcome here—but I've got to say you look a mite peaked." I wasn't sure what peaked meant, but I'm sure I looked it.

Kyle grinned and said, "That's Millie for you, she'll tell it as she sees it—sort of bossy like a mom or sister."

We ordered a pot of coffee and sweet rolls, and I excused myself to 'the john.' I splashed cold water on my face, combed my hair etc. and felt somewhat better, then made my way back to our table.

Quite a crowd had gathered around listening to Kyle, and no doubt hearing about how he had met me. They all had serious expressions on their faces, ranging from sympathy to fear.

One man patted me on the back and said, "Congratulations Allen you're dang lucky to be alive cuz some didn't make it past that bridge."

They all wanted to have a detailed account of what had happened to me and I needed to know what that fellow was talking about. There was dead silence as I took a big drink of coffee and looked at my watch. I explained I wouldn't mind talking about it, but I had an appointment with the owner of 'Abe's Now and Then' store around 4:30. I really needed to save a little alone time to get my brain back into the business mode.

I said, "I'll be back here around 6:15 and have the hamburger special and I'm sure I'll feel more like talking and eating by then. I'm not heading back to Houston tonight since it will be too late, so I'll check into a motel after my meeting. Anybody wanting to hear my crazy tale is welcome to come back—. Fair warning—it makes no sense." Most all the guys said they could be back and wouldn't miss it. They equally had my curiosity up and I needed to know more about that 'bridge of terror.'

I took another drink of coffee and started to get up when one of the fellows named Thomas walked over to our table.

He said, "They should put a warning sign up a few miles before that damned bridge—with something like: 'put the pedal to the medal'."

Thomas shook my hand and promised to come back later. He said, "I'll bring a friend, if he's up to it... Poor guy had a horrible experience with that bridge—and what lurks beneath it."

I'm sure I had a puzzled look on my face as I wondered about that ominous statement. I hoped Thomas' friend had an explanation or clue to what had happened to me. Whatever Kyle had told these people, they seemed very understanding, like my wild tale was not that unusual around this town. For sure, there was no way I would tell anyone what happened to me when I got back home. Even my uncle, Big Boss might think I needed a vacation to the 'funny farm.'

I finished off a sweet roll and coffee as I listened to them talk about a variety of things. I went back to 'the john' and freshened up for my meeting and told Kyle thanks again and I would see them later.

When I got back in the car it took me several minutes to settle down. After my near fatal accident and hearing 'spooks' calling to me, it would be hard to act like business as usual, but I would give it my best.

I was a little early for my appointment, so I took the opportunity to look around this country styled department store. One section had antiques and collectibles, and the other all your modern day needs. I was wondering how one person could manage two completely different businesses as this under one roof, and then I got my answer. A man dressed in the eighteen hundred's style of clothing came up to me and asked if I was Mr. Allen Franklin. I answered yes.

He said, "Welcome to our 'Now and Then' store. I'm Will Scott. I handle the antique section and my uncle owns the store. He manages the 'Now' half, and he's the one who contacted you. Follow me please."

Will Scott said, "This is Allen Franklin and this normal looking fellow is my uncle, Abe Scott."

Abe Scott smiled and said, "My nephew likes to dress to match his furniture, guess I should wear a tall hat like old Abe Lincoln."

I was thankful for their relaxed manner since my day had been everything but.

He said "You know, I still like to meet the person I'm dealing with at least once rather than shopping on line or by phone, so I appreciate you coming out here to the 'boondocks.' By the way, did you have a nice drive here?"

His question was not unusual, but my expression and delayed answer must have given me away. As lightly as possible I said, "Well I got sleepy on the way and almost collided with a bridge."

Will said, "Are you talking about the bridge just before getting into town?" My answer was—"Yes, that was the one."

He replied, "You're fortunate to be here talking to us. Within the last twelve years there have been eight deaths by that horrible bridge."

Mr. Abe added, "Needless to say no one has any idea of how many near misses, but I bet there have been a lot. Our local newspaper editor has published some pretty bizarre stories over the years, not counting the normal death notices. Sorry, Allen, I didn't mean to upset you more than you probably are already—just thought you should know a little more about that bridge."

I could have told them there was a lot more than a bridge that had brought terror to me that day, but maybe they already knew that. Just thinking about the cries for help—and those strong icy hands on mine trying to force me off the road, gave me the shivers.

I said, "Sorry Mr. Abe, I didn't mean to get us side tracked about my misadventures, and I want you to know I do appreciate your information. Since it's getting a little late in the day I am seriously considering getting a motel for a night or two." I told him I would leave a catalogue and samples to look over and would give him a call the next day.

Mr. Abe and his nephew, Will, shook my hand and said they understood and thought that was a good idea.

Mr. Abe said, "A good friend of mine has a nice motel a couple blocks from here called 'Charlie's Rest Well Inn.' It's not fancy but the rates are good and it's clean."

After thanking them again, I gave Mr. Abe my cell phone number and said I would check in at his friend's place. That was the best decision I had made all day, especially since I had no reason to rush back to Houston tonight. I checked into my room, showered and then headed down the road to the café where my 'new found' friends would be waiting for more of my wild story. Hmm, I thought, what an odd way to get new friends.

First things first, I was going to relax with the hamburger special and a beer. I was surprised to see so many vehicles there and wondered where they would seat all those people. I hoped they hadn't come here mainly to hear my tale because that would be a little embarrassing. As I walked in all eyes were on me and I fussed at myself thinking, "Dang—maybe I shouldn't have been so eager to come back here." Oh well, it was too late to turn back now. Besides, I needed some logical answers—if there were any.

Kyle greeted me with a smile and handshake and said, "I told all these folks you weren't saying a word about what happened to you till you got a good meal under your belt."

"Thanks, that sounds like a deal." He then led me to a table. I felt uncomfortable getting a seat while so many others were standing around. It was pretty clear they were here to see the guy that lived to tell about 'it.' It being the 'Bridge of Terror.'

Millie, the waitress, smiled as she said, "The boss says yours is on the house, and that's the least he could do since you sure brought in extra business." How funny, I thought! Now I really felt like I was on display. I thanked her but figured I wouldn't enjoy my hamburger after all, not with being the main character in the 'upcoming show.'

Kyle changed the subject as he asked me how my meeting went. I told him, just fine and how friendly Mr. Abe and his nephew were.

He replied, "I've never been in the store but I did meet the nephew in here once—nice guy."

I told Kyle and the others at the table that I planned to stay one or two nights at Charlie's Inn since I had no reason to rush back to the big city. Besides, after my ordeal, my mind and body needed some rest. They all agreed that was a smart idea... I glanced around at the people talking and eating in their small groups, but I could sense an air of anticipation among them.

Our food arrived and it didn't take long for me to see why their hamburgers and onion rings had such a great reputation. As I was gazing around the room at these folks, all heads turned to see who was entering. It was two fellows, and one was Thomas, the man I had met earlier who suggested the bridge needed a warning sign. I figured the other must be the friend that had experienced something far worse than I had. Thomas held the door open as the fellow maneuvered his walker in with some difficulty. He was probably in his late sixties, but the painful look on his face with each step he took made him appear older. Many shook his hand and greeted him warmly as he was guided toward the table where I sat. I stood up like the rest to greet this celebrity of sorts.

Kyle introduced him as Lucky Bill, and the fellow managed a grin and said, "Well from the looks of me—I couldah been more lucky."

Thomas said, "Well, Allen, guess you could say I'm Lucky Bill's angel, like Kyle is yours."

The waitress worked her way through and said, "Sit yourself down guys—will it be chili and beer as usual?"

They each nodded and Thomas said, "Yep—Millie, you got it!"

Lucky Bill sat down at our table and his friend Thomas, sat in back of us, leaving one empty chair. I smiled at the thought; hmm maybe, they are leaving that one for the mayor. Everyone continued with his or her eating and small talk. I glanced around at the packed café, and was a little surprised to see Mr. Abe and his nephew Will walking towards our table.

With big smiles and outstretched hands, Will said, "Word gets around fast in a small town, and we didn't want to miss hearing your story."

They made their way to an area where they could at least get something to drink and still hear. I'm thinking, this thing sure is getting out of hand, but maybe it is the only way I'll ever half-way understand what happened to me and the others. Guess it won't be long before they will want old Lucky Bill and me on stage. Just as I'm thinking this café won't hold another person, a tall man came in carrying a briefcase and walked directly to our table.

Kyle said, "Allen I hope you don't mind me inviting Joel Hadley to listen to your story; he's the editor of the newspaper here. I filled him in on the parts I had witnessed, and told him you would tell the rest tonight. Needless to say, 'wild horses' couldn't keep him away."

I stood up and shook his hand as we were formally introduced. I muttered, "Well, what the heck, for whatever it's worth I'll tell it, just don't use my last name if you print it."

"Thanks Allen, just call me Joel. As you see we are all an informal bunch around here, so I'll get right to the point. " He continued on, "I started working with the Bull's Eye newspaper a little over six years ago, that was just before the seventh mishap occurred. When you learn about the ordeals others went through, you will understand why there is so much interest in what you have to say. There have been eight deaths at that bridge in twelve years and they all happened around this time of the year."

Lucky Bill was nodding his head as he said, "It only takes men, and I think I know why."

Another person said, "Yeah, even one of those goofy people from a magazine came here. You know, the kind that tells about someone being taken to Jupiter in a flying saucer for experiments or something."

Kyle called out, "Everyone please settle down so Allen Franklin can tell about his experience with our 'bridge of terror.'"

You could have heard a pin drop as I cleared my throat—and with a nervous voice I began my strange tale. "I'll stand up so you can hear me better, but evidently you have heard several weird tales like mine before. My drive was fairly normal till shortly after I left the town east of here, then things started taking a turn for the worst. I seldom get sleepy driving, but today was totally different. I couldn't keep my eyes open no matter what I tried, like lowering the windows to let fresh air blow in my face and turning the radio up. I saw a narrow logging road, pulled in there and walked around the car a couple of times, but had to move on as a big truck was coming toward me. When I got back on the main road, I immediately became uncontrollably sleepy again. I couldn't think straight and felt like pulling over, even though there was no place to safely do that. I noticed the logging truck was no longer following me even though I had seen no other side roads. It felt like something or someone was trying to control me—. Suddenly a freezing blast of air filled my car and if that weren't crazy enough I started hearing moaning sounds—. Sorry, guys—I need to stop a minute to catch my breath and get a drink of water." As I did, I looked around the room filled with people listening to this outlandish tale—and I couldn't believe it was me telling it. I noticed Lucky Bill with his head face down resting on his arms, as if to hide from some unseen evil.

He looked up and said, "We're safe now, buddy—so go on and get it all out in the open."

I thanked him and said, "You are right, Lucky Bill—here's the rest of my nightmare. The car seemed to be vibrating with cold air and moans pounding in my head. As I got closer to the bridge they clearly turned into a mournful 'help me, help me' over and over. I saw heavy skid marks leading to the concrete bridge, and I knew some unseen force was pulling me towards it. Sounds crazy, but I could feel strong icy hands on top of mine trying with all 'It's' might to do just that. Guess that's when I really started praying to God for help. You could say God sent Kyle and his loud horn just in time, and I'm sincerely thankful for all three. Well I think that's all of the crazy details—just hope I didn't disappoint you folks." I could tell by their expressions that I hadn't and was surprised when they all stood up and applauded me... A stranger, with an even stranger tale, at least it was to me. I was greatly relieved to get it off my chest though I knew I would never get it out of my head.

Kyle gave me a pat on the back and said, "I was so thankful that I was there to help. Funny thing, I hardly ever take that route, but decided to drive it today."

Joel Hadley took out a laminated sheet from his briefcase and said, "Folks, Allen needs to hear this, so I'll read part of this twelve year old article about the first death that occurred at the bridge. Allen, this information will possibly give you some clues to the why and what of your near accident. There are no logical answers to how anything like this can happen, so we just reason the best we can."

Here's the article. "Mr. Jake Pardue, a native of this county, died in a tragic accident at the Green River Bridge. He had hauled logs many years for The Ted Gaberson Lumberyard, and was an outstanding employee. He was working a double shift on that fatal night, so it is reasoned he may have fallen asleep at the wheel. When he failed to return to the lumberyard at the expected time, his family and friends checked everywhere, but no accident had been reported. He and his truck were reported missing—but sadly —were not found until two and half days later by a fisherman."

Joel said, "This is from a separate article quoting what the fisherman, Josh Duvall, had to say about the Pardue incident." "Ah parked near duh Green River Bridge jest hoping to ketch some big catfish. Ah started down them steep banks, Ah sees deep tire ruts heading fer der water. Them bushes and little trees were all pushed over, that's when Ah saw a logging truck on its side at de edge of duh water. Ah got no car phone, so hurried to der sheriff's office."

Joel, the editor, said, "This is part of the sheriff's report." "We arrive at the scene with necessary equipment and, not too far from the truck, we found the body of Mr. Pardue. It was in shallow water with a log across his legs. The recent rains had caused a slow but steady rise in the river. Had this not been the case, Mr. Pardue may have survived the wreck because the autopsy showed drowning was the cause of his death. With sadness, it is believed his demise must have been a slow and painful one. He will be greatly missed by his family and friends. May God rest his soul."

I am sure my face was a little pale when Kyle asked me, "Well, Allen, what do you think about that poor fellow and how it fits in with your story?"

"In the past my reaction to a ghost tale such as this would have been to laugh it off, but now I'm not so sure."

Joel remarked, "I once read an article telling how this kind of phenomena might happen. It said that when a person dies tragically or suddenly, an essential part of their energy could linger on earth. This might manifest itself in a ghostly form or exert other powers, especially if that person had unresolved issues.

Lucky Bill raised his head and said, "I don't rightly understand all them words, but poor Jake Pardue can do all those things, cause I felt and heard him and sorta saw him."

Millie, the waitress called out in a in a loud voice, "Would anyone like coffee or something before Bill tells his spook tale?" It sounded like everyone said yes at the same time, so she and the other waitress took orders.

This gave me a few minutes to reflect on the goofy la la land I was in, but at least I shared it with a room full of understanding people. With coffee cup in hand, I felt I was as ready to hear his grizzly tale as I ever would be.

Lucky Bill took a deep breath and said—"If you don't mind I'll just sit while I talk. It was two years and six days ago that I ran off that dammed 'bridge of terror'—which I might add, was about this time of the year. My elderly uncle was in the hospital in the next town over, and I had sat up with him all night. The next morning after breakfast I headed home thinking how glad I would be to get a little shut eye. I started getting sleepy almost right away but after being awake all night, that was understandable. Out loud I said, "My Lord, home's not that far away so surely I can stay awake that long. Like Allen I tried wind in my face and loud music, but nothing helped." With a pause he stated, "You people have heard my tale but Allen hasn't, so I better tell it like it was. Not too far from Green River Bridge, I noticed a log truck in back of me, but next time I looked it wasn't there. Even though I could hardly keep my eyes open and my mind straight, I knew it hadn't passed me. A big blast of ice cold air hit me in the face and that jerked me wide-awake big time! It felt like my pickup had turned into a freezer. I knew for sure I'd gone crazy, cause I started hearing someone moaning to boot. It got louder and was plainly saying 'help me' over and over. Allen, I know this sounds just like your story and up to a certain point it is. That was one hell of a spook trying to take over us. I'm a strong guy, but those icy hands on mine were controlling the wheel and making me head toward the bridge. Like you I saw black skid marks and was thinking enough to apply my brakes. I missed the concrete part but I ran down the embankment."

Lucky Bill gave a shiver and stopped talking for a moment as he relived his terrifying experience. He took a long drink of coffee, and that's when I saw how pale he was getting. His friend, Thomas, was sitting at the table in back of us, and he stood up and put his arm around Bill's shoulder to calm him down, and said—"It's okay fellow, you're safe now."

Bill cleared his throat and looked directly at me, then began where he left off. "I had gotten in a hurry that day and didn't have my seat belt on so I was thrown out of my truck. When I came to, my head was bleeding and hurting something awful, but even worse was that one of my legs was trapped under the truck. I had landed in the deep mud at the edge of the river so that probably saved my life—. You understand these are thoughts I have now, and not what I was thinking at the time of the accident—or for a long time after. It was a total nightmare because I was hearing, 'HELP ME, HELP ME,' booming in my ears. Sounded just like someone was next to me. I was hollering as loud as I could, but I'm sure in a weak voice, and this unseen person sounded louder. In a daze, I'm thinking—we sound like a ghostly duet. I could hardly move, but I saw a strange, cloudy shape close to me—and it kinda rose up and down. I'm thinking—please God; don't let me die here like old Jake Pardue. I put all I had into a cry for help and then passed out."

"You rest now Lucky Bill," urged Thomas. "Since this is where I entered 'the picture,' I'll take it from here. Hopefully, Bill hadn't been lying under his truck too long before I arrived at the scene. I slowed down when I noticed a curl of smoke coming from under the bridge, but just figured a hobo or fisherman was cooking their dinner down there. However, about that time I heard a muffled cry for help. I parked on the other side of the bridge, and hurried down the embankment. There was a pickup on its side at the edge of the water with smoke coming from the hood. I prayed to God that that whoever was inside wasn't hurt too bad. The river was fairly narrow at that spot, so I could see no one was behind the wheel—however, the windshield was busted out. Quickly I climbed back up, crossed over the bridge then back down that side to get a better look. While doing this I called 911 on my cell phone. I was breathing heavy but I managed to tell them to get to the Green River bridge ASAP because there was probably someone in bad shape—or worse. For once I was glad my wife made me carry that silly cell phone. I remembered her saying that someday I'd be glad to have it. Well she was sure right!"

"So back to Lucky Bill's horrible nightmare. It was plain to see by the broken windshield that someone had been thrown out, and as I walked around the side that wasn't in the water, I found this poor fellow. There was blood all over his face and head and his leg was pinned under the truck. I glanced around but didn't see any other bodies alive or dead. Kneeling down beside him, I checked to see if he had a pulse, and, praise the Lord, he did. I had a clean handkerchief so I wiped the blood from his eyes. I was saying a silent prayer for him when his eyes fluttered partly open. I'll not forget that wild stare he had as he pleaded, 'Stop—stop—I can't help you!' I gently patted him on the arm and told him not to be afraid, because I was going to take care of him and more was on the way. However, he was most likely out of his head with pain so he probably didn't understand me.

"About that time I heard an ambulance and fire truck heading our way, so I climbed up to the road and waved them down. I hoped this other person he was talking to wasn't lying dead somewhere. Whatever the case, I'm sure a thorough search would be made if this fellow was unable tell us about this 'other person.' As I led the medical crew down the slope, I mentioned the fellow seemed to be talking to someone else when he woke up, but he was the only person I had seen. We discussed this accident and how many victims this damned bridge had claimed, six to be exact, but for the moment at least, this one was still alive."

"As we approached, he opened his eyes and tried to tell us something but it didn't make any sense. One of the medics asked him if there was anyone else traveling with him and he surprised me by saying—'No!' That was a big relief and one less thing to worry about. The men in the fire truck and two guys with a wrecker were busy hooking the truck up so it could be raised without doing more damage to the fellow's leg."

One of the medics said, "I think this is Bill Stephen, a friend of my uncle's. They are both veterans and like getting together to eat and talk over war times. I met him once while they were eating at the Corner Café, and it was hard to say what they were doing the most of. He lives by himself on the outskirts of town so I don't know of anyone we should notify."

Thomas continued with, "They figured this Bill Stephen had a concussion, so they couldn't give him anything to ease the pain in his leg – but made him as comfortable as possible. I turned to the poor fellow lying there in the mud mingled with blood, and held his hand. I hoped he could understand me with all his hurting when I told him, 'Bill you're gonna get over this, and we can get together anytime you want and tell some war stories.' He gripped my hand like he understood so I told him what was taking place, and then moved back out of the way."

"Apparently the crew had gone through this type of procedure several times, because it wasn't long before they were hoisting his truck up. There were a few tense moments due to the muddy banks, but they got it back on the road. Once the vehicle was off this poor guy's leg, the medics secured him and carefully carried him up and eased him into the ambulance. All this time Bill was moaning and semi-conscious I guess, because he sure was talking out of his head."

"One of the medics was looking through his billfold for any information that might be needed and found his V. A. hospital care card. I asked if they would be taking him there because I would like to follow along in case he needed someone with him. They said yes and thought that was good for me to be with him. Just be sure to keep a safe distance from the ambulance."

"Guess I took Bill on as my special project and now we're best buddies. The doctors were as concerned with his mind as with his mangled leg, but after a few months they dismissed him."

Bill spoke up, "Yeah, Thomas, remember they saw I wouldn't back down on my story so they gave up on that part." He continued by saying, "Well, Allen, I enjoyed meeting you and hearing your story. Just sorry old Jake and his bridge of terror tried to get you too." Turning to Thomas, Bill said, "Would you mind running me home as I'm pretty tuckered out."

I patted him on the back and said, "Lucky Bill, I'm real proud I got to meet you and 'your angel.' Thanks again for coming and helping to shed some light on my puzzling and frightening experience."

Even though he had suffered injuries, I understood why people called him Lucky Bill. As he and Thomas left the crowded café, everyone stood and gave them a big hand. It was good to see and feel the support these folks were giving him and me. Over the years they must have heard some strange stories regarding this ghost under the bridge.

Most of the people began filtering out, but not before shaking my hand, wishing me safe travel and hoping I would visit their town again.

Millie, who had been intently listening said, "Ditto, just come the other way."

The newspaper editor, Joel Hadley, said, "Maybe the by-pass will be finished soon and that will make it closer and safer."

"Oh," I exclaimed, "How long has this been in the works?"

Joel said, "At least five years, and if you can meet me in the morning, I'll fill you in on that plus 'bring you up to speed' regarding our infamous Bridge of Terror. The Bull's Eye newspaper, where I work, is just off the square, to the left as you come into the main part of town. While you're there I'll show you the 'morgue' or in plain talk, the old news articles about the bridge."

I was anxious to learn all I could about this crazy phenomenon or whatever you want to call it, so my answer was, yes.

Joel then asked, "Would you like to meet at the Corner Café on the square around 8:15? I'll treat you to breakfast. No offense intended to this café, but that one is closer to your motel as well as my work place.

"Sounds like a good deal," I replied, "But I feel I should buy yours since you are taking up your Saturday on me."

"Don't worry about it, Allen, just think of it as a business expense, and, of course, it's a pleasure."

Joel told me, "I plan to write a short article when I get home, about your almost tragic accident and have it ready for you to proof read it in the morning. He assured me that even though my story was similar to the others, people would want to hear about Jake Pardue's yearly attempt."

I stood up and we shook hands and I said, "See you tomorrow."

Kyle remarked, "This has been quite a day for you hasn't it, Allen? Bet you're pooped out." I couldn't have said it better myself, and knew it was time to make my way to the motel before I 'crashed' on the spot.

I turned to my new and very special friend and said, "Kyle, words can't say how much I appreciate everything you have done for me, with number one being saving my life. Who knows, maybe we'll see each other again and anytime I have business here, I will definitely come by this café." We exchanged cell phone numbers and promised to keep in touch. Just as I was telling the other folks good-bye, Mr. Abe and Will approached me and told me how sorry they were about the bad experience I had undergone that day.

Mr. Abe said, "I would like to place an order if you feel like staying a little longer, that way you wouldn't have to stop by the store tomorrow."

"Thanks," I replied, "That is very kind of you and, quite frankly, I need to get my mind back to reality."

He said, "I'm sure you feel like you've visited a ghost town today, and are more than ready for some peace and quiet. I have the order form filled out so the transaction shouldn't take long. I like the unique designs of the table lamps and other accessories, plus your prices are good." After all the details were taken care of and a few more handshakes, I was out of there.

It was only a mile or so to the motel and, brother was I ever ready to 'crash' ― into a bed, that is! Though it wasn't late, it felt like midnight. I was very grateful to get inside my safe, quite room and had hopes of getting some much-needed sleep. This day had been absolutely crazy, so I had my doubts about sleep, even though I was dead tired. As I stretched out on the comfortable bed and stared into the darkness, my mind started replaying the events of the day. I tried comforting myself by the assurance that I was unhurt and it was over. At least, I had certainly met a bunch of kind, understanding people—otherwise I might have been taken to a psychiatric hospital or the morgue. I tossed and turned and finally drifted off, but not where I wanted to be. My nightmare began where the daytime one had left off. First it seemed my car got caught in an icy whirlpool, then I was sucked out of it and dumped onto the muddy riverbanks where many hands frantically reaching out to me. I couldn't tell if it was Lucky Bill's or one of the more unlucky fellows. In my 'dream sleep,' I was pleading with them to leave me alone, when one voice became more distinct. "Help me; help me the water is rising!"

Suddenly I was startled out of my nightmare by a loud radio in the motel parking lot and for once, I was thankful. I exclaimed out loud, "My Lord, I was dreaming of old Pardue himself!" As I looked out the motel window, I saw one of Charlie's employees 'reading some kids the 'right act.' With the radio booming and tires squealing, they took off to bother someone else. If I'd had the chance, I would have thanked them and given them a twenty-dollar bill. That would have really freaked them out. Whatever, I thanked God, I was out of that rotten dream. I propped myself up in bed and started watching some old movie, and the next thing I knew my alarm was ringing. Well, at least I got a few hours of rest and after showering, I was ready for a good breakfast and whatever Joel Hadley had to show me.

When I arrived at the Corner Café he was already there having coffee and talking with some of the locals. He greeted me with a friendly smile, introduced me to a couple of the people, and then they went to their own table. Great! I was not ready for another session like last night. Joel asked how I slept, so I told him about my stupid nightmare. After that our conversation was more down to earth as we enjoyed a country style breakfast. He told me some interesting things that he had done before coming to this town and what he does in his spare time. I in turn gave him a brief 'rundown' on what I did.

"Well Allen, guess it's time to head over to my office and get down to business."

When we entered the Bull's Eye newspaper building, there was a pretty redhead sitting at the front desk that welcomed us with a smile.

He said, "This is Rebecca, my right hand lady—. Rebecca, this is Allen Franklin the latest survivor of The Bridge."

"Oh—my—gosh! Joel, I wondered what would bring you to the office on Saturday, now I know... Sorry, Allen—that wasn't a nice welcome to our little town, was it?" Before I had a chance to answer, she said, "Allen, I will be looking forward to reading the latest saga on what Joel has to say about "The Bridge of Terror" and your experience."

Joel replied, "We will be busy in 'the morgue' for awhile Rebecca, so tell the cleaning people not to worry with that room this week."

As soon as Joel closed the door behind us, I blurted out, "Wow, what a great looking lady—is she spoken for?"

Joel just smiled and said, "I'm glad to see your head is on straight after the crap you went through yesterday. Rebecca is not only a beauty; she's good about coming in on Saturday mornings just in case we have some 'breaking news' to take care of... Even though this is a pretty small town, believe it or not, we do have a few noteworthy things happen besides our annual bridge of terror tales. I say annual because, as you heard, there is a definite pattern. Like most people, I figure the years not accounted for just means there was a 'near miss' like yours and that person took off like a bat out of hell—. I'm sure I would want to get as far from there as possible."

I agreed with Joel's comments and said, "Maybe their 'guardian angles' broke the trance they were in, like mine did."

Little by little all of this unreal stuff was starting to sink in, and it left a knot in my stomach that I knew would remain for a long time.

Joel handed me the article he had written about my frightening experience. Reading it through, I complimented him on the excellent way it was explained. We sat down at his computer and he went to the file labeled 'Bridge.'

He said, "I'll not read the first one about Jake Pardue since you heard it last night. These next articles are about the fatal accidents that occurred at the bridge in the following two years. As mentioned before, three factors were present in all incidents. They involved men drivers, this time of the year, and no known cause for the wrecks. The fourth year after the Pardue incident, we have nothing, but that could have been one of those near misses. Year five and six brought two more deaths. By then people were sure that Jake Pardue had put some kind of curse on that bridge because it was too much to be just a coincidence. Pardue was a respected and well-liked man when alive, but evidently something had changed in his death process. Whatever the case, when folks can't find a logical reason, they blame things like this on some evil presence. From your experience and the others, it is easy to see why."

I listened intently as Joel continued on to year number seven. "Millie, the waitress, called me saying I needed to get to the café ASAP because the bridge nearly got someone else. She said the couple was pretty shook-up, but would talk with me if I got there soon. Needless to say, I hurried to the café."

Joel looked up as his receptionist/reporter, tapped on the door. She poked her head in and said, "Allen, would you like a Pepsi, water or coffee? Joel ~ guess you want the usual? With all this serious talk, you may need something stronger... Well Allen?"

Joel broke the silence with, "Allen, are you going to have Rebecca use her mental-telepathy, or—do you plan to tell her what you want?"

"Sorry," I stammered, "I would like a Pepsi." I blushed as I said— "Guess my mind was somewhere else.

"Like heck!" Joel said, and then laughed.

Rebecca blushed a little and said, "You silly guys!" She smiled and said, "I will be right back so Allen can get his mind back to—the history lesson."

Joel said, "She's right, we better get back to the story at hand. When I arrived at the café, Millie was talking to a lady and a man. The guy looked pretty shook up, and was holding onto his coffee mug like it was a security blanket. We were introduced, but I'll just call them Mr. and Mrs. X. I thanked them for their willingness to talk about what happened, and I briefly filled them in on past events. I assured them their real name would not be revealed—as I guaranteed you."

Another little tap at the door and Rebecca was handing us our drinks. Smiling as she remarked, "I'll not bug you ghost hunters anymore."

Joel commented, "Hmm, Allen, I don't think you mind getting bugged, do you?"

Without thinking how silly it would sound, I said—"Bug on ladybug!" Then quickly added, "Sorry, Rebecca—I don't know where on earth that came from." She just laughed and shook her head as she left the room.

"Back to 'ghost hunting, Allen... Their stories were quite long so naturally for the newspaper article, I condensed them greatly. To make their tale more meaningful, I'll let you hear what I recorded."

With a shaky voice, Mr. X began his story; "We had been traveling most of the day so we took turns with the driving, that way we don't get too tired. It was my time to take over while my wife napped, and since we were only two hours from home, I would finish it out. I was thinking about all the things that I needed to do the next day when I suddenly became very sleepy. Since I had slept just before we had eaten lunch at the last town, I couldn't figure why my eyes were so heavy. I thought wind blowing in my face would make me feel more alert, but it didn't."

At this point Joel stopped the recorder and said, "Allen to save time, he basically heard and felt the same things you did, even saw a logging truck that apparently vanished. When he finished his frightening story, his wife gave him a hug and took over the conversation."

As Joel turned the recorder back on he said; "This is Mrs. X talking now."

"I was jolted from my nap by the sound of squealing brakes and the jerky car movements. I screamed out, 'Roy, what's wrong?' With horror I saw we were heading towards the bridge, so I grabbed the steering wheel from my husband who seemed to be in a trance. The car swerved just enough to miss hitting the bridge. My husband snapped out of 'it' enough to apply the brakes. He was pale and talking out of his head so I thought he was having a stroke or something. I told him I would drive to the next town and check him into the emergency room. As I drove, he began calming down a bit and said he didn't hurt anywhere and didn't want to go to the hospital. Roy told me to stop at the first place we came to that would have coffee or whiskey; then he would try telling me about the crazy things that happened to him. I just figured he must have dozed off and had a nightmare."

Joel turned the recorder off again and said, "I was hired as editor of The Bull's Eye and moved to this town just a few months before Mr. X became number seven of the 'Bridge of Terror' mess. Those first months I had familiarized myself to a certain degree about the 'Bridge' that plagued this town, but this was different hearing about 'it' first hand."

With a serious look on his face he said, "That was my first time to investigate anything of this nature—however, I had done some research on the subject of paranormal happenings. This definitely fits the description of paranormal!"

Joel told me 'off the cuff,' once Mr. and Mrs. X relaxed, that he thought they enjoyed being the center of attention. He then turned the recorder back on and said, "This is Mrs. X talking again. I only printed the necessary parts of this in the newspaper article."

"I saw this café and pulled into the parking lot, and was glad it wasn't at a busy time, that way we would have more privacy. Maybe my husband could explain his strange actions and wild tale. When we entered the café we were greeted by the manager, I guess, because he told us to sit wherever we wished and Millie would be our waitress. I chose a table near the back so we could talk without everyone hearing us. Soon Millie, the waitress, came to our table and asked us how we were doing today and I replied—well the bridge just down the road nearly got us, but I think we're okay now. The waitress looked shocked and cried out, 'My Lord not another one!' She apologized to us for her strange sounding remark, and her next one was also puzzling, because she said it was a yearly event around there. Millie, the waitress, asked if we would like something to drink while we settled down from our ordeal. I told her we would like two black coffees and two cinnamon rolls, and then maybe we would feel better.

Sarcastically, Mr. X spoke up, "Well—dear, since this is MY spooky story you sure have done all the talking." He shook his head and murmured, "Least I know I'm not the only crazy person around here. I guarantee we will never travel this way again, regardless of the time of the year."

Joel turned the recorder off and said, "Enough on those characters. Next we go to the eighth and ninth years when two more men met tragic deaths beneath the bridge. The newspaper and local radio station had a big splash on these very unusual accidents. I'll not forget the visit I had the day after I had written a lengthy article and brief history on the 'Bridge of Terror' incidents. Ms. Laura Gaberson, a highly respected lady and owner of the Ted Gaberson Lumberyard, came bursting into my office."

In a demanding voice she told me, "Joel, this has got to stop before our town's image is completely ruined! I understand one of the television talk shows was discussing our town and said they had proof the Green River bridge was haunted and possessed by poor Jake Pardue." She felt it was probably one of those people who survived the bridge, and got paid big bucks to be on television. I politely agreed with Ms. Laura, as most everyone calls her, and told her I had seen the show and I felt she was right on all counts. After that I had also noticed more strangers in town. Allen, before I go further with her complaint and plan, I'll tell you a little about her. Really she is a super fine little lady and without her interest in this town and its people, this would not be such an outstanding place to live. Ms. Laura has been a widow for a couple of years, and even though she doesn't have to go to the lumberyard, I hear she checks on things there at least once a week. By all accounts she looks on her employees at the lumberyard as family, so this whole sad episode has been extra stressful for her.

Ms. Laura said—"Joel, turn your tape recorder on because I have an important plan to tell you about. I have been thinking about that terrible bridge for several years, and since the problem is not going to go away on its own, I am ready to take drastic measures! This is my plan... Tuesday I am going to the city council meeting with my ideas and wondered if you would go with me. After that, I am planning to consult with a good friend who works at the capitol in Austin."

I asked her, what kind of solution could there be, since we have no control over supernatural or unnatural things.

Without hesitation she said, "I will have them reroute the road, do away with that bridge and build another. I own all the land around there and I will gladly give the county or state what they need. If they need matching grants, I will definitely help with that too... Now Joel—can I count on you to help me?"

"Allen, I knew it would not be as simple as Ms. Laura had planned, but what the heck, so I told her I would do whatever I could. First we would need to convince the 'right' people that this section of road was hazardous, or why else had such a large number of deaths and accidents occurred at the Green River Bridge. No doubt most people had heard or read of the strange events surrounding the deaths there, but perhaps they would think logically and assume possible human error, road or weather conditions as the cause. We would not hint of any paranormal activity. Ms. Laura said we would concentrate on the bad curve in the road. Well, Allen, there was one delay after another, but when that little lady sets her mind to do something, it gets done eventually. Since there were no landowners to bicker with, that would speed things up a lot."

Joel said—"Let's get back to the yearly count down on that cursed bridge. After the eighth death, there was a deluge of news and other media people around town seeking any bit of information they could get their hands on." Flipping through a folder he pulled out one of the pages and said, "Allen, the following story was told to me by a fellow around that time; this might give you an idea about the atmosphere around here."

He said, "My buddy, Jed and me was a fishing at Green River when we saw some folks down under the bridge in a circle. They was talking weird like one of them spooky movies. Jed and me figured they were trying to contact the dead with one of them séance things. Whatever they were trying—guess it didn't work."

Joel said, "Hope I don't 'lose' you, Allen, with all this 'switching' back and forth... Okay—back to the more logical approach suggested by Ms. Laura. We made many phone calls, wrote letters, and made two trips to Austin. If it hadn't been for Rebecca and my crew, the newspaper would have been in trouble. It was and is a very worthy project, so I did what I could. It's also a good thing Ms. Laura had the funds to match her determination—now back to the story!"

"Ms. Laura and other town people were really raising cane with the Texas highway department about the long delay. Finally it was officially announced that all of the paperwork was completed, the new route surveyed and the bulldozers would be there in a week. Everyone in town was overjoyed."

Joel finished off his bottle of water, and then got back to the long tale. "Roadwork was actually started a few months before Lucky Bill almost became a statistic for year number ten. The eleventh year the bridge, or Jake Pardue's ghost, claimed a young fellow's life that had just graduated from high school. Several of his family and friends commented about him always being a safe driver so they couldn't understand how this had happened to him. Allen, this makes your near miss year twelve. You're the third person on record that was nearly killed at the bridge with year four unaccounted for. That is a total of eight tragic deaths.

The new road and bridge should be ready within three months, so your story will surely be the last on this Pardue ghost mess."

Just then Rebecca opened the door and with a mocked bossy tone said, "You guys need to take a lunch break."

Joel said, "Well, Allen, you see what I have to put up with?"

I thought, lucky you! But my reply was—"I should get back to the motel and get my stuff together. I figure I will head back to Houston after I get a bite to eat... Believe me—I will definitely take the longer route to I-45 just in case old Pardue wants a second chance at me." I surprised myself by saying, "Ah—Rebecca would you have lunch with me?"

Joel laughed as he said, "Are you trying to steal my good help away?"

With a red face, I'm sure, I said, "Please excuse me, Rebecca, I'm not normally so blunt."

Rebecca put her hand on my shoulder and said, "I'm sorry I can't take you up on your offer today. Perhaps we can make it another time."

With my usual charm— (HA!)—I tried to re-coup by casually saying, "I should have known a beautiful lady like you would already have plans."

Rebecca burst forth with laughter—and then with a serious tone she replied, "Allen, my evening will be anything but romantic since I'm taking my elderly aunt to lunch and shopping."

I stammered slightly—"Well, I promise, I shall return and hopefully I won't put my foot in my mouth every time I open it."

Again!" Rebecca flashed a beautiful smile and said, "I'll be here, Allen."

"Great, I'll get back here as soon as I can—spooks or not!"

Joel and I exchanged phone numbers and he promised to keep me informed on any future events regarding the 'bridge of terror.' I knew the people from this area would be greatly relieved to see the old bridge demolished and for the unsuspecting traveler like me, doubly so. However, even if my business didn't take me to this town, I planned to find an excuse to visit here. That excuse was Rebecca. I fussed at myself by saying, "You silly nut, we only said a few words to each other and you acted like a complete klutz."

My drive back to Houston went smoothly and the plane trip home also. Thinking about my nightmare weekend helped pass the travel time, but I still felt like I was trapped in one of the "Twilight Zone" movies—as I mentioned earlier. However, I must say meeting that cute redhead was special, just wish I hadn't made such a fool of myself.

Three weeks later I had an unexpected call from Joel Hadley, the newspaper editor. He said, "I have some good news and some sad news. They were putting the finishing touches on the bridge before it would be officially opened, when one of the workers decided he would take his lunch break by walking down to see the Green River Bridge one last time before it was demolished. When he didn't return after a reasonable amount of time, a couple of guys went looking for him. They found him under the bridge dead. Perhaps old Jake Pardue's ghost figured this would be his final chance since he had been cheated out of his last victim... We must have really 'teed' Pardue off. That marks the death of nine fellows in twelve years."

"The good news is the grand opening of the road and bridge will be next month on Saturday the 14th at 2 PM. I sure hope you can be here as we plan to have a big get together at the community center afterwards. Oh—before I forget, Rebecca told me to give you her phone number—in case you wanted to give her a call. Really can't imagine why she would think that," he said with a laugh.

Joel continued on with, "Seriously now, here's a hush-hush item. Ms. Laura told me a few years back, a friend had suggested to her, that she should hire a certain professor, who might possibly get rid of this 'ghost thing.' After reading a book about him and his accomplishments, she decided we should seek help from this highly respected parapsychologist. At first she had hesitated calling this Mr. H. since he lived in New York and might not want to travel this far on a possible 'wild goose chase.' However, the way the last death occurred, we were afraid these tragic deaths might not stop."

Ms. Laura told me, she would try calling him that night to inquire if he would consider coming to our town, and if he thought it would be possible to put poor Jake Pardue's ghost to rest. She blushed and said she felt quite silly saying that—but maybe Mr. H. wouldn't think so. The next day she came to my office in a very excited mood to tell me about her interesting conversation with this person and his unusual profession.

Ms. Laura said, "I was surprised when Mr. H. told me he was familiar with the 'Bridge of Terror' incidents and had wondered about them over the years. He said he mainly goes where he is invited—so 'it' had been 'placed on the back burner.' Besides teaching, Mr. H. and his medium stay busy traveling around the country and sometimes abroad, helping other desperate people. Since I didn't know what a medium was, Mr. H. explained it was a person who went into a trance and often could sense or speak with a deceased person, and sometimes the spirit would speak through them."

Ms. Laura told me the following, "Mr. H. was willing to come and bring his crew, so a date was set. He suggested we should meet the following year in May around the time of Jake Pardue's death, since that was the most likely time something might occur around the bridge. Mr. H. cautioned me to tell no one other than you, Joel, since I had been confiding in you and possibly one other person that we could trust to help with the set-up. If word got out on this, it would be useless to pursue." Sternly Joel said, "Now Allen, I feel you are trustworthy plus being a bridge survivor, so you will be one of the first to know what happened—if anything. If Mr. H. and his medium resolve this Pardue situation, we will have a big celebration soon afterwards. That is almost a year away, but knowing the importance of this will make the secret easier to keep. In fact, I swore Rebecca to secrecy since she will be included in this ominous venture.

I told Joel he could count on me to keep the secret—and how much I appreciated his trust. Hopefully there would be a 'farewell celebration for Jake Pardue'—if so I would definitely be there.

He said, "Allen, I almost forgot to tell you what the bridge will be called. Everyone wanted it to be 'Laura's Bridge,' but she insisted it should be called 'Peace Bridge'—so that's what it will be."

I thanked Joel for filling me in on the news about the dedication of the new road and bridge and especially the prospects of getting rid of

Jake Pardue's ghost. I told him to tell all the people I had met at the Top Spot Café, that I would be there on Friday and Saturday for the bridge dedication for a reunion' of sorts.

Casually I said, "Tell Rebecca I'll call her tomorrow and fill her in on my future plans—. Oh yes, do you remember my eighteen wheeler friend, Kyle? Have you seen him lately?"

Joel said, "Yep, what kind of reporter would I be if I didn't remember that his loud horn saved you. He was by this way once since you were here, that I know of."

I remarked to Joel, "I have his cell number so I'll let him know about the new bridge dedication, in case he hasn't heard. He told me he would try to arrange his loads so he could be in your town sometime when I'm there." Actually, I was glad to have a reason to be going back to that little East Texas town. In fact, three or four reasons. The new bridge, new friends, a good client and best of all—Rebecca.

I called her saying I would be there for the celebration of the new 'Peace Bridge.' She sounded happy to hear my voice and said she would meet me at the Top Spot Café Friday night around 6:30 for dinner.

Those three weeks passed quickly, and I found myself heading back to that little town I secretly called "La La land." I went twelve miles out of my way—even though it was not the month old Pardue was active. I figured the new bridge wouldn't be open till tomorrow and I sure as heck didn't want to chance the old one or possibly the spook under it.

When I pulled into Charlie's Inn parking lot I was glad I had a reservation, because the sign in front read No Vacancies! After checking in, I called Joel and Rebecca to let them know I had arrived and would see them in a couple of hours. I thought to myself, "Allen, be cool! Don't blow your chance with Rebecca this time!

This weekend promised to be a blast with dinner tonight with Rebecca, then breakfast with Kyle, my trucker friend and later meeting another very special lady, Ms. Laura. From what Joel had told me, she's got to be the coolest, 'go-getter' around. Even though she wouldn't allow the bridge to be named after her, I felt sure she would be honored in many ways.

I had time before going to the café so I called Mr. Abe and Will just to say I was in town for the bridge dedication and they asked me to drop by, which I did. I had a nice visit with them as we discussed a variety of things, some business but mainly about the Green River Bridge being replaced.

Will remarked, "I'm certain everyone in town will be at the bridge dedication, because it's the biggest deal this community could possibly have. It's been awful for our town to be known as the 'Bridge of Terror' town for so many years. "

As expected, there was a big crowd at the Top Spot Café that Friday evening. I was greeted by a big howdy and hug from Millie as I looked around for an empty table.

She said, "Hey man, we got a reserved table for you and your group. Isn't it great that we're getting rid of that damned Bridge of Terror? Don't know what we'll talk about, les it's who's running around with so and so."

"Good grief girl, that subject will be a big relief to everyone, except Pardue," declared Lucky Bill. "Do you think he'll start bothering the people fishing or the smooching?" Those remarks got Lucky Bill some big laughs.

There were familiar faces in the café, but I wondered where my more special friends were. Just then Joel and Rebecca came through the door with outstretched hands and big smiles. Hmm, I thought Rebecca and I were down for a date, not Joel and others at the same table.

Guess I looked a little worried as I remarked, "Joel, hope this pretty red head isn't your date—oops, I did it again!"

They both laughed heartily, and Rebecca said, "Allen—I see you still have a bit of the foot in mouth' problem—but that's okay! Remember—I said I would be happy to have dinner with you. We can sit at the little corner table."

I knew my face was red as I stammered, "Well, Rebecca, I guess you both have seen how uncool I can be."

She told me, "Allen, don't worry, I think it's cute."

Hum—I thought—maybe cute is better than stupid. Joel just stood there laughing and enjoying the silly show we were putting on. It was a fun evening, and sitting next to this pretty lady made it doubly so. Time came to say the goodnights and see you tomorrow stuff, and goofy me, goofed-up again. Rebecca planted a simple 'peck' on my cheek and if I had been 'on the ball' I could have turned quickly and gotten an even better kiss.

The next morning Kyle, my trucker friend, met me for breakfast and a few tall tales. He told me he was sorry he would be unable to be there for the new bridge dedication, since he had a rush job. After a brotherly hug I told him to take care out there in 'that wild rat race.'

He said, "Right! Allen, you watch out for those bridges." We both laughed even though it was really no laughing matter.

I drove back to my motel, wrote in my journal, took a little nap and then walked to the Corner Café for lunch. I wished I had thought to ask Rebecca to meet me, but at least I would get to see her later on that day. I told myself if we lived closer to each other, maybe we could really get something going—if she wasn't already involved with someone. I remembered how friendly she was last night, so maybe there was a possibility something could develop. Funny how 'tangled up' I was getting with this little town and its people, all because of a ghost guy and a bridge.

Back at the motel, after freshening up, I relaxed in front of the 'tube' while waiting for Joel to pick me up. Not much on, so my mind wandered to last night's conversations. Rebecca mentioned the city manager had rented several buses in order to cut down on traffic to the new road and bridge. They would shuttle people from the community center by bus to the ribbon cutting and tour.

Around 1:30 there was a tap at my door and Joel called out, "Hey man, are you ready? Rebecca and I decided we needed to leave a little early or we might not get a seat on a bus." Joel pushed a pile of papers etc. to the other side and said he hoped I didn't mind sitting in such a messy back seat. I assured him I was used to that.

Rebecca flashed a nice smile and said, "Well, Allen, we certainly have 'wall to wall' traffic today. Looks like everyone for miles around has come to the bridge dedication."

Four busses were parked at the community center and someone had made large banners for each bus saying, "Welcome to Peace Bridge Road" and below it a slightly smaller one with Ms. Laura's Bridge.

Joel pointed out the stretch limousine that was parked in front of the busses and said, "Ms. Laura and the 'city fathers' are in it and you can be sure it wasn't her idea." Joel parked and we got on bus number three. There were only aisle seats left, but that was better than getting in the long line of individual vehicles.

Not far out of town we came to a 'Y' in the road with detour barriers across the new road. We sat there while several men in a pick-up removed them and placed them at the side of the old road.

Joel explained, "After we make the final 'loop around' today, the old road will be blocked to the Green River Bridge leaving only a small gravel road for people to get to the river to fish or swim."

I had a good feeling when I read the new sign, Peace Bridge, and I'm sure the folks around here were shouting for joy. There was the usual ribbon cutting, a few speeches, then back in the vehicles and driving across the new bridge. We then followed the parade of vehicles looping around for the last crossing of Green River Bridge, alias the Bridge of Terror.

I commented where others could hear, "No fear of Jake Pardue venturing out with all this traffic." Everyone clapped!

Back at the community center I got the privilege of talking with Ms. Laura, and she was not only clever, but also a real sweetheart.

When Joel and Rebecca took me back to the motel, I told Rebecca I would call her when I got back home—if it wasn't too late.

She said, "Allen—call it won't be too late." Hmm, that gave me a boost! As we parted I sneaked in a quick hug and thought to myself—what a firm body and nice perfume.

"Ah— hope I'm not intruding here," Joel said.

I 'paid' Joel back by saying, "If you don't mind—I'll just shake your hand." We all had a good laugh. I thanked him again for keeping me 'in the loop' about events taking place in this great little town. He promised again, that he would call with results on the Mr. H. deal regarding the Pardue curse.

I will skip the details that took place in those next nine months or so, but I will say everything progressed well, even a few dates and a big phone bill with Rebecca. Now I'll fast forward to when I got the important call from Joel about the meeting with the parapsychologist, Mr. H.

Joel was so excited when he told me, "The 'séance' type meeting with Mr. H. was successful—and unreal." He added, "Rebecca gave me the privilege of letting you in on this news first. Course I had to treat her to a steak dinner—you still planning to be here for the results?"

I quickly said, "Absolutely!"

He said, "Great! Ms. Laura, Rebecca and I are firming up details for the 'grand finale' of Jake Pardue and The Bridge of Terror' saga. I'll have an article on the front page of my newspaper and also put an announcement on the local radio station about the meeting. It will be in the school cafeteria because there is bound to be a huge crowd present."

I could hardly wait to hit the road to my favorite little town and hear about this strange experiment. At least, that's what it seemed to me. After my plane landed at the Houston airport the dark clouds started building up. That would be great weather for a ghost story but not being in the air, so I was thankful 'it' waited.

When I pulled into Charlie's Inn, Charlie himself greeted me. With a big smile he said, "Howdy, Allen. Welcome to your second home. Glad you called early cause everything for miles around is full up. Lots of strangers are interested in that killer bridge... Don't need to ask why you're here."

"Well Charlie, I'm sure you know both reasons." I called Joel to let him know I was in town, and he told me to hurry over because a certain someone was asking every thirty minutes where I was. I was doubly anxious to talk with Rebecca in person, even though we talked every other day—I had something special to tell her.

The swirling, greenish gray and black clouds were forming an ominous net over the town and they looked ready to explode any minute. Had it not been for that, I would have walked since it was only a few blocks to the school. It was almost two hours before the meeting would start, but traffic was already bumper to bumper. There would be no spots near the school so I whipped over the shoulder and parked safely off the road. Grabbing my umbrella, I took off in high gear. My goal now was to beat the rain there. I barely did!

People were parked everywhere possible, waiting for the doors to open. I was glad I had parked down the road. All eyes seemed to be on me as I boldly walked up to the door. It was locked and a sign said, "Will not open doors until 4:00 PM." I knocked anyway. Joel's voice sounded a little stern as I heard, "Yes—? Sorry—can't you read?"

"It's Allen Franklin, Joel—does that mean me too?"

"No Allen, hurry in before the stampede starts." Quickly glancing around, I saw Ms. Laura and Rebecca placing sandwiches and drinks on a table—so that's where I headed. There was a large cake in the center that read, IT IS OVER!

I didn't waste any time greeting each of them with a hug, and needless to say one was quite a bit more personal. I told Rebecca I needed to have a word with her when she had time.

Ms. Laura said, "You go on dear, I'll finish up here."

Hand in hand we walked to a quite spot, and I told her the good news. "You remember me telling you that I am 'the Little Boss' and my uncle is the 'Big Boss?' Well I talked him into the idea of me moving to Houston. It would actually save us quite a bit of money, you know airfares, etc. and besides I would be more centrally located. We handle almost everything by computer or phone as it is anyway."

Rebecca's face glowed as she exclaimed, "That's great Allen! We can have a long talk about it after the meeting."

The doors were opened and the people poured in. Joel welcomed the overflow crowd and said, "Great to see so many of you folks getting out in this rotten looking weather. With a topic such as this, however, I'm not surprised. Believe me this program will be well worth braving it. I will get started right away and hopefully we can finish before the storm hits. Afterwards Rebecca will cut the cake and then feel free to visit as long as you like. Ms. Laura and I will try to answer any questions to the best of our knowledge, which is pretty limited in the paranormal area." We followed Joel's directions, as we were all anxious to hear what took place a little over two weeks ago. Most of the people didn't have a clue to what the meeting was about other than it had to do with Jake Pardue's curse on the bridge.

The weather was certainly helping to set 'the stage' so to speak, as the lighting and booming thunder let us know we were in the middle of a pretty severe electrical storm. Some people were getting a little edgy and several said they hoped the lights wouldn't go out. Joel and

Rebecca found a couple of flashlights and a large box of candles just in case they were needed. They placed them around the room and had matches handy. Joel told us not to worry if the power went off because his tape recorder had fresh batteries and we would at least be able to hear what happened. It definitely would be spookier in the candlelight.

Joel said, "Ms. Laura will tell you about the special person, Mr. H., that put a closure to the terror that has taken place at the Green River Bridge. This Mr. H. had me video part of it, which I'll show after the tape recording is finished—if the lights stay on."

A huge crash of lighting sounded like it hit nearby, causing quite a commotion. What timing! We were in total darkness. Rebecca turned the flashlights on and with the help of others lit the candles around the room. Joel said, "Some of you people will need to move closer in order to hear." When all settle down Ms. Laura explained how she had chanced upon Mr. H., as we will call him. She told a little about his most unusual profession, which is a parapsychologist. He had purposely chosen the time and day of the year the tragic 'accidents' had occurred. Her last remarks on that subject was, "I had utmost confidence him then and now—a reason being—it worked!"

There were a few nervous laughs as Joel announced, "The show will go on, and perhaps the lights will be back on before we leave." Joel filled the others in on what he had previously told me, and then asked everyone to please have an open mind because what they were going to hear, and hopefully see, would be pretty weird. He also asked for complete quiet while the recorder was on because some of the sounds were almost a whisper. Between the unusual opening statements—and the terrible weather, everyone was glancing around at each other—wondering what would be next.

Joel continued, "Okay—on the appointed day, Rebecca and I picked Ms. Laura up and drove to the airport in Houston where our unusual guests were waiting. Mr. H. introduced himself and the lady with him, as his medium, Sara. He told me that I could print their real names only after he approved the story. Mr. H. also said it was okay to record anything I wished, so I did. Ms. Laura Gaberson, Rebecca and I had a lot of questions regarding the type of cases they had dealt with and Mr.

H. willingly gave several examples. Their stories were very interesting, to say the least."

Joel continued on, "Mr. H. had told Ms. Laura in one of their phone conversations that we were not to mention anything about the Green River Bridge or Mr. Jake Pardue in the presence of his medium, Sara. He wanted her to go to the scene and 'pick up' things on her own with no pre-conceived ideas. Ms. Laura had simply told her housekeeper that these were some kin people visiting for the night. We didn't want a word of this to 'leak out.' A word to leak out. We packed a folding table, chairs, water and of course my tape recorder in the van that night. With an air of excitement, I picked up Rebecca, my helper, and the others the next morning and we headed down the new road and crossed over the Peace Bridge. At this point there was very little talking, which was partly at Mr. H's request."

Joel stopped for a drink of water, and then continued on. "The lady he had brought along seemed agitated and began shaking her head like she was trying to wake up. I kept driving but managed to turn on my recorder—just in case something interesting was said. What Sara was going through was a little distracting—however, we were giving a sign not to speak to her. As we approached the area where Jake Pardue's truck had left the road, Mr. H. had to calm Sara down. In a soothing voice he said, 'Don't worry everything will be all right.'"

Joel said, "The Bridge was no longer intact but, as you know, the highway people had left a small access road from both directions for folks who like to fish or swim there. I parked my van where it would be out of sight of any curious town's people. Mr. H. had some unusual looking electronic things that we would need to carry, so I parked as close to the death scene as I could."

There were a few small screams and other comments as a deafening clap of thunder vibrated through the school cafeteria.

"Wow!" Joel said, "That was close, guess Jake is still mad at us. Sorry folks, I shouldn't have said that. Everyone, aquatinted with him when he was 'in the flesh,' knew he was a fine fellow.'"

Okay, back to the story. Mr. H., Rebecca and I carried the chairs and card table to a level spot near the area where Pardue's body was found. Next we placed the electrical equipment near where Sara would sit. Mr.

H. and I turned our recorders on—sure didn't want to miss anything. I went back to help Ms. Laura, as the ground was uneven—and of course she gave me one of her special looks and said she could do it blindfolded.

All joking stopped when we saw the expression on the medium's face and the frantic way she was moving her arms around. It looked like she was having a huge problem. When I turn the recorder on for you folks to hear—I will speak softly and only to explain what is taking place.

Mr. H. said in a whisper, "Sara will be all right when this is over. She is already feeling the deceased person's presence—or perhaps he has temporarily taken over her body."

Joel continued, "Ms. Laura and Rebecca sat down and I went back to help Mr. H. get Sara down the path to where the chairs were. By that time she was moaning loudly—and the sounds that came from her throat were those of a man. I'm glad our recorders were running and on the table, where they could pick up this strange voice. Mr. H. asked me if I could operate his video camera since his cameraperson was unable to be there. I was happy to help and pleased that he trusted me to do so. Rebecca took notes. It wasn't easy getting Sara seated, because it was as if she couldn't hear or see us."

Mr. H. whispered, "She is in a trance now so I will 'guide' her the rest of the way. Please remain silent no matter what takes place."

Joel turned on his tape recorder and said, "All right people, it's time to hear what my recorder picked up. You will hear a husky man's voice coming from this petite lady. The calm voice belongs to Mr. H."

"Sleepy—oh NO—NO—can't stop!"

"What is your name?"

"Can't stop—can't stop!"

"Who are you?"

"Pardue—Jake Pardue! Help—gonna crash. Oh God—truck's rolling over." (Silence) Moaning. "Help me—help me!"

There were gasps throughout the room. This was the voice of their old friend, Jake Pardue.

Mr. H's calm and gentle voice—"Yes I will help you—where are you?"

"Legs under logs—can't you SEE?"

"Are you in the water?"

His ghostly voice burst out, "Hell yes—need help—waters rising! Help me NOW!"

Mr. H. asking, "Has anyone stopped to help you?"

"Ugh—They don't talk to me!"

Softly Joel said, "Remember all this time Mr. H. was talking with Pardue, through the body of his medium, Sara. It was super strange! At this point Mr. H. gently put his hand on her shoulder—but was speaking to Pardue."

He said, "Jake Pardue, I am going to help you now. I am deeply sorry you have suffered for so many years—but please trust me and your suffering will be over."

The gruff voice that came from the mouth of Sara was startling, "What? —Years—what you mean YEARS?"

Sympathetically, Mr. H. replied—"Jake, your body died many years ago, now you must leave this spot of torture and look to the light where your loved ones are waiting for you."

"No—no! Can't be—I'm here—sounded his frantic voice."

"No, Jake, you need to move on. Only painful last memories are holding you here—. It's over friend—go in peace."

At these words, Sara, his medium relaxed and sighed—"Did anything happen?"

Mr. H. said, "Yes, thanks to you and your remarkable gift. It seems we have helped 'free' another trapped spirit."

Joel turned the recorder off and told us the rest of this strange tale. "If I hadn't seen and heard what took place, I wouldn't have thought it possible. I'm here to tell you, the whole thing gave me goose bumps."

Ms. Laura exclaimed, "Well I had goose bumps on top of my goose bumps! It was like being in some horror movie watching the ghost of a dead man take over that lady—. Poor thing, somehow her whole appearance changed as her voice did."

Rebecca nodded in agreement and said, "That's a big ditto."

Ms. Laura continued on, "Mr. H. told us he truly felt Mr. Pardue had at last made his journey to the other side where he belonged. He would be no further threat to anyone—so if there were accidents around the new bridge—that is just what they would be. We thanked Mr. H. and Sara for coming to our rescue. They only asked for a transportation fee—but of course I gave them a little extra. It was such a sad thing to hear, but I'm sure our old friend Jake did not realize he was causing other people to die there."

Joel said, "Whatever the case, I think we should give Ms. Laura a big hand for her persistence in getting rid of that deadly problem."

I chimed in, "And for all of your help!" We sat there in the flickering candle glow and our applauding drowned out the claps of thunder.

Lucky Bill, who was sitting on the back row, cleared his throat and said a loud, "Amen!"

Everyone had sat spellbound as they listened to the dramatic conclusion of the local ghost that had resided under the Bridge of Terror for so many years. Suddenly everyone began talking at once—like a floodgate had been opened up. It was the sound of many relieved people.

Perfect timing! The lights came back on so we were able to watch the video, which made the wild story more complete and believable.

Someone said, "Let's make a farewell toast to Jake Pardue—and that blankedy—blank 'Bridge of Terror.' We had no Champaign but decided coffee and Pepsi would work just fine.

Ms. Laura said, "Rebecca how about cutting the cake to top off this very special evening."

I snuggled close to Rebecca and whispered—"Later will be even more special—Sweetie!"

*****

"I Remember When"

I remember when I was a teenager, my best girlfriend's name was Doris. Even though it has been over sixty years ago, I recall the many fun times we had. Unless you grew up in that era, you probably think we didn't have much to do with no technical things like television, computers, cell phones, hand held games and "the like" around, but perhaps we used our imaginations more... Come to think about it, some of those things were invented by my generation!

One of the more unusual things we did was to publish a monthly neighborhood newspaper. My brother was the editor and did a great job of it. Of course, that was when people knew everyone within a block or two and were more interested in their neighbors. Another different thing we did was put on plays in one of the neighbor's garages. Since there were no electric dryers, there was always at least one clothes line in part of the garage to use in rainy weather. An old sheet or two made a nice curtain. Doris and I usually wrote the script and make sure everyone had a part that wanted one. An added plus was—that she had a cute older brother. Sometimes he agreed to be in one of our plays and I would manage to give him the part playing my boyfriend. He didn't take the hint—sorry to admit—but he never seemed to have any romantic interest in me at all. Oh well, as we said then—"Que' Sera, Sera"—which means, what will be will be. Since this isn't about some silly teenage crush, I'll get on with my tale... Actually—it's a pretty spooky one.

Doris and I made a point of spending two or three nights a month with each other and in the summertime even more. One day her mom called my mom to invite me to spend a weekend with them in Galveston. She said, "We will be staying at our kin people's house which is near the beach, so I'm sure the girls will find plenty of fun things to do there."

Since our parents knew each other well, Mom said, "Sure—just don't let them keep you up all night with their talking and giggling."

I was so excited you would have thought I was going to Paris. The next morning I was waiting on the porch as Doris and her parents drove up in their black Chevy.

Her dad hollered out, "You don't want to go to Galveston, do you?"

Mom came out and said, "Betsy could hardly eat her breakfast, and said she would just die if you all had decided not to go."

"You're right Mom! This is going to be soooo fun!"—Sadly, however—I noticed my 'secret crush' was not in the back seat.

Doris saw that fleeting look and said, "That brother of mine just had to go to a baseball game. Guess we won't have to worry about him sneaking up and hitting us on the arm. I hate when he does that and then laughs. Guess that's one of those silly guy things."

We crossed over the long causeway. Lucky there wasn't a ship coming in or it would have been a long wait. Back then there was a bridge that raised up to let the boats go through.

Naturally the windows were rolled down since their car had no air-conditioner, and besides, we wanted to enjoy the smell of the salty ocean breeze. I told them, "I think Galveston would be a neat place to live— EXCEPT in hurricane season." They all quickly agreed with me.

Doris' dad asked, "Do you get to come here very often?"

"Not often enough. Mom and Dad take us kids here two or three times a year to play in the water while they fish—but I know this time is going to be different!" I just didn't know how different it would be.

Doris and I talked and talked about all the fun things we hoped to do.

Her Mom asked, "Did Doris tell you anything about the kin people we're visiting?"

"Ah—no, except that the people were old and lived in a big old house not too far from the seawall."

"Well, that's true. Their house has two and a half stories and was built in the early 1900's after the big hurricane. The last time we saw it, it needed quite a lot of work but, don't worry, I know they keep it clean. One other thing—my aunt and uncle that live there, takes care of her mother who is almost bedridden and seldom speaks. The doctor says her problem is dementia but my aunt thinks she understands more than people realize."

Doris' dad told us, "In plain English—it will be best not to make a lot of loud noises around her as it might frighten her. Other than that, we know she will be glad to see some young faces. They all will."

About that time he pulled into a circular driveway. The house was tall and narrow with vines covering a big part of it and—yes it sure was old. In fact, most of the houses on that street looked the same, and all were very close together. In a whisper I asked Doris, "You suppose they have any ghosts haunting their place?"

"Heck if I know! I've never spent the night here. In fact, I was only here a few times before. Mom and Dad came more often than us kids—guess we found something more fun to do, like spending the night with our friends... Hey, Betsy—do you want to have a séance?"

"Nope, not me—and don't even think about using a Ouija board! Hmm—did you bring one?"

"No, silly! Mom wouldn't have let me even if I had thought about it... Remember what happened at Karen's party?"

"Yikes! Yes too well—! That goofy thing moved by itself."

Doris' dad said, "What is all that whispering about? Never mind explaining your 'girl talk.' Time to get out and see how these folks are doing."

We were greeted warmly by their aunt and uncle as Doris' Mom introduced me to them.

Her aunt smiled and said, "Betsy, so nice to meet you. You may call me Aunt Jewel if you like." Before I could answer, the uncle laughed and said, "Well, you can call me Uncle Dale—even though I'm old enough to be your grandpa."

I told them I would be happy to have an extra aunt and uncle.

Aunt Jewel said, "I need to check on Mother in the kitchen. Dale will show you all to the living room. Make yourselves comfortable. I'll be back shortly."

There were a several stuffed chairs and two couches facing a big fireplace and that's where Uncle Dale motioned for us to sit.

He told us, "We make fires in here almost every winter because rooms with tall ceilings like this are hard to heat."

Doris' dad said, "Boy, we sure don't need it today—good thing you had some ceiling fans installed. Must be near a hundred degrees today."

Aunt Jewel walked in and said, "Amen to that. Follow me upstairs and I'll show you where you will sleep. After you get situated we can sit and talk in the kitchen where Mom is."

We followed her up the creaking stairs as I glanced at Doris and whispered, "Booo!" She snickered.

Her aunt said, "Doris and Betsy, this will be your room—I thought you would prefer the twin beds, and if you want to listen to music, there's a radio." We thanked her and placed our small suitcases on a folding furniture rack. I had never seen one so Doris told me what it was for. I checked the rest of the room out and then walked to the window. I pushed the pretty lace curtains apart so I could see out better and said to Doris, "Someone around here must do a lot of yard work, like my dad. Lots of pretty flowers in the back yard... Oh—I see an old fellow with a hoe so he must be the one."

Doris said, "Well, hope he doesn't get too hot." I looked again and he was gone so I figured he had found a shady spot to rest. We decided to check out the yard and the rest of house. Doris said she knew her aunt and uncle wouldn't mind. However, by the time we got down stairs, the rest of her folks were in the kitchen having lemonade and cookies, so we joined them.

Aunt Jewel smiled and said, "Betsy, this is my mother, Mrs. Emma, but you may call her Granny like most folks do. Doris, I think you were around ten years old when you were here last; in fact, it was at my daddy's funeral. Do you remember that?"

"Yes, I do. There were lots of people around but Granny still found time to talk to me." Doris walked over to the kitchen table where this very old lady sat staring into space. She leaned over and gave her a kiss on her wrinkled cheek. "Hi Granny—I'm Doris." I saw a couple of blinks from her pale blue eyes—and then back to the blank stare.

Doris and I sat at the big round table enjoying cookies and lemonade while the grownups talked—and Granny stared. How sad, I thought, to end up so helpless.

I turned to Aunt Jewel and asked, "Would it be alright if we took some lemonade to the old fellow working in your back yard?"

All heads turned my way, even Granny's! I got some strange looks and noticed how pale Aunt Jewel's face was... I wondered why.

Uncle Dale was the first to speak, "Betsy, there's nobody working this yard but me. Guess you just saw a shadow."

Shadow "my foot"—I thought to myself. Maybe it was a bum messing around out there pretending to be working. Whatever—he looked solid to me.

The subject was changed with no further discussion about what I thought I had seen.

Doris' mother said, "I'll take you girls to the beach now if you like." I think we both answered at the same time, "If we like?" In no time we had changed into our bathing suits, got our beach bags and hurried to the car. She warned us, "Don't go out past your waist because the waves and undercurrent can knock you over—AND don't fall for those fast talking guys—if there are any around. Your dad will pick you up in two hours—so be right here."

I shook my head yes and Doris said, "Sure! Sure Mom we promise. We'll try to resist all those flirty guys, just hope there's some around."

We had fun jumping the waves and picking up shells—but the most fun was watching the people going by. Namely the good looking guys showing off their tans and muscles. Two of those were following three girls with blond hair. They were all pretty skinny except for their 'boobs' so Doris and I figured they must be stuffed with socks. We had a good laugh and guessed they would be safe—if they stayed out of the water.

A couple of hours later we heard three short honks and Doris said, "That's my dad, right on time." We dusted off as much of the sand as possible, spread our towels on the seats, and climbed in.

He grinned and said, "Well, bet you two cuties turned a few heads."

"Dad! Don't be such a teaser. The truth is most of the guys were only interested in the peroxide blondes."

I shook my head in agreement and replied, "Doesn't matter—it was fun anyway."

We chattered and sang on the way to their aunt and uncle's place and her dad just smiled at our "silliness." Soon we were back at their house and after a quick 'hi,' we headed for the showers. I love the beach but I don't love all the gritty sand. "Yuck!" After freshening up we joined the grownups in the kitchen for lunch where all but Uncle Dale were seated around the table. "Hmmm, it sure smells yummy in here!" I said.

Doris gave her aunt Jewel a hug and said, "Yeah, thanks a bundle, we are about starved to death." That brought a big laugh from everyone. Except, of course, from Granny. About that time Uncle Dale walked in and declared, "Whatever the laughing is about, we need it around here." He blessed the food and we all had a great time eating and talking.

We offered to help clean up the kitchen but Doris' mom and aunt told us to shoo along. Doris told them we planned to walk around the block and checkout the shell shop on the corner. Her mom told us to be careful and, of course, we promised we would. Parents, at least ours, were always reminding us about that—even though I don't recall any bad things happening around where we lived.

Our walk was interesting and we each bought a few shells at the corner shop even though we knew they weren't from Galveston.

Big thrill! We got 'wolf whistles' from a couple of guys in an old convertible—so I would say it was a pretty exciting walk.

Back at the house, I told Doris I wasn't convinced it was a shadow I had seen in the back yard and would like to check out the area. I stood in the spot where I thought I'd seen the old man, and it wasn't close to any trees that could make a shadow.

Doris said, "Maybe it was a ghost! You know that book we read about Galveston last year said there were lots of haunted places in this town—. Ah—nah—probably just your wild imagination."

"Don't make fun! Maybe it was someone real—or maybe it WAS a ghost."

We went inside the house and listened to the grown-up talk for awhile then back to the kitchen to have supper. They had leftovers but Doris and I had peanut butter and jelly sandwiches. After a while we headed to our room and listened to our favorite radio program, "The Inner Sanctum." About an hour later her dad tapped on the door and told us it was time to 'hit the hay.' Actually the bed did look very inviting—more than a bed of hay would have. Actually it had been a busy day—and we were 'pooped out'—so with little talking we drifted off to sleep.

Sometime later I was awakened by a hand on my back. With a jump I said, "Yes, Doris, what is it?"—There was no answer. I looked over to where Doris was sleeping and she was lying still with her eyes closed. Weird, I thought to myself. Must have been dreaming—but I didn't know something in a dream could give a person goose bumps. I drifted back to sleep. It didn't seem like much time passed before I was startled awake again by a cold hand on my shoulder. My eyes flew open and there was an old man staring down at me. Chills were racing up and down my whole body as I screeched out, "Who—who are you?"

Doris flipped the light on and said, "What the heck are you hollering about?"

"Ah—ah —an old man was standing by my bed just staring at me."

"Betsy, you 'goofball,' no one is in here except us—you were just dreaming."

"NO WAY! He touched me on the back two times! But—you must be right—he couldn't just disappear. Or could he? Come to think about it, he looked like the man I saw in the back yard. Maybe it was a ghost.

"For 'Pete sakes,' Betsy—let's get back to sleep. There's not a thing or person in here that's going to hurt you. Boy—I didn't know you had such spooky dreams."

"Me neither," I sighed. However, to myself I thought, I know it was a ghost... "Doris—is there room for me in your bed?"

She laughed so loud I thought she might wake up her folks. She said, "I'll make room, you scaredy-cat."

I rolled on my side facing the bed I had been in, and Doris faced the other way so we had enough room. Soon I could tell she was sleeping—but not me.

I could hear the old grandfather clock chiming in the hall every fifteen minutes so I knew what time it was. About an hour later the bed we were on seemed to rise up a little—like someone was getting out of bed. I was fully awake when I saw a wispy cloud like thing form into an old man. It was the same old man that had scared the heck out of me earlier. I softly tapped Doris on the back and whispered in her ear, "Shhh—turn over slowly and look at my bed." Without a word she did as I told her.

We both stared in amazement as the ghost of an old fellow gently patted the pillow, then turned around and headed back to the bed where we were. "Yikes!" we both squealed as we jumped out of bed and ran down stairs. When we got to the living room, Doris pointed to a picture on the wall and said, "That ghost was my Grandpa."

We spent the rest of the night curled up on the two couches in the living room. Our plan was to go back to our room when it started getting light—but we didn't wake-up in time.

Aunt Jewel found us there. "Why on earth are you girls sleeping downstairs?"

Doris paused and said, "Aunt Jewel—please don't think we are just a couple of crazy teen-agers—but we saw the ghost of Grandpa in our room last night."

She looked a little pale as she sat down between us. "Girls, I'm so sorry you had such a fright—please tell me what happened."

First off I was surprised because she didn't laugh at what Doris had blurted out. I said, "Okay—truthfully—this is what happened." I told her exactly what took place and Doris added the parts she had seen. Aunt Jewel nodded her head in an understanding way.

She told us, "My mom and dad used to sleep in that room after they had gotten older. Mom had painful arthritis and it was easier to get out of the twin bed. Dad would check on her all during the night, and apparently his ghostly body still does that. Betsy, the bed you were in was Mom's and Doris you slept in Dad's. I think we both shivered and said "Brrr!"

Just as we were finishing our scary tale Doris' mom and dad walked into the room with good morning greetings. They could hardly believe we were already up. Before we could explain why, Uncle Dale came through the hall pushing granny in her wheel-chair. In a cheerful voice he said, "Top of the morning to all yew landlubbers." His expression changed when he saw our serious faces.

Aunt Jewel rose to her feet and with a smile she said, "Let's all go to the kitchen and have some sweet rolls and coffee. You girls can have juice and milk if you like." After we were all seated she said, "Dale—Betsy and Doris have discovered our little secret, so we might as well get it out in the open."

Doris' mom and dad had puzzled expression on their faces, and their Uncle Dale just shook his head.

She continued with, "Betsy, please explain to the rest of the family what you girls saw last night." Again I told the spooky story and Doris chimed in every so often—mainly the part about when the ghost started to get into the bed with us. I glanced toward Granny and it was plain to see she was trying to speak at least with her eyes.

Aunt Jewel walked over and gave her mom a hug and said, "Mom, you know how Daddy used to get out of bed off and on during the night checking on you—? Well—he is still thinking about you."

Her mom had a slight smile on her face and a tear ran down her sweet wrinkled face. In fact, everyone in the room shed a tear or two.

Uncle Dale said, "Yes—and he still works in the back yard, and he never looks tired. Sorry I fibbed to you, Betsy." I just smiled and said, "That's alright—I sure understand why." Without a doubt this was one of my most special "I Remember When" stories as a teenager—and still is.

*****

"The Tower That Breathes"

"Some Facts with a Measure of Fiction"

The tower I'm writing about is located in the lovely historical town of Port Isabel, Texas. It is The Point Isabel Lighthouse.

Before I get into my story, I'm including a few interesting things about the lighthouse and its location. Later you will see why, because some have a direct 'bearing' on the scary experience that I encountered inside the lighthouse walls.

In 1851 Port Isabel was chosen as an ideal location for a lighthouse. Not only would it serve to guide ships with its beacon light, it would be a good observation post to protect the docked ships and businesses along that area. In the earlier days Pirates often posed a threat.

Construction began in 1852 and was completed in 1853. The beacon light was first lit April the 20th of that year and was extinguished between 1888 and 1894. In 1905 The Point Isabel Lighthouse was decommissioned since most cargo was shipped by railroads. However, the lighthouse has never lost its special place as a beacon to residents and tourists.

The Point Isabel Lighthouse served an important position during the U. S./Mexican confrontation, the Civil War and World War I. It would have been hard for an enemy to enter into the port under the watchful eyes that patrolled along the 'cat walk' (the upper railed off section) of the lighthouse. Strangely, both Confederate and the Union armies used it for an observation post.

There was once more than fifty lighthouses lining the treacherous shores of Texas, but at the time of this writing, there are only five remaining. The Point Isabel Lighthouse located next to South Padre Island is the only one open to the public. With those historical facts (as best I know them) in place I shall get on with my rather spooky tale.

Quite by accident, I discovered there seemed to be an energy force (not in flesh form) that dwells within the earthen walls of the Point Isabel lighthouse. Perhaps it could be a lighthouse keeper from over one hundred and fifty years ago or a soldier from the Civil War days. Needless to say they each would have taken their jobs very seriously since it could have easily been a life or death situation if they had not.

Now for a brief explanation about me and why the interest in lighthouses. For many years one of my hobbies has been painting on canvas with seascapes and port scenes being my favorite subjects. When suitable, I've included a lighthouse to add extra character. There are two small, rather unimpressive ones near the Gulf coast town where I lived, but I would add the more dramatic ones from other locations. Until recently, I had not been to the South Padre area so I wasn't familiar with the Point Isabel Lighthouse.

Many years have passed and, though I still love to do art work, I am now devoting more time to my writing. I told my two daughters that I planned to write about a lighthouse and wished I could go inside one in order to get the real feel. We each started looking online and discovered (as mentioned) Port Isabel is the only one in Texas still open to the public.

Rebecca, the daughter that was able to go with me, said, "April would be a great time to fly there, but not during Spring Break."

My younger daughter sighed, "That lets me out since the kids will be in school."

I reassured her saying, "Laura, if it's a fun place with lots to do, maybe we can all go there on a summer vacation."

"Sounds like a plan! I'll remind you later Mom."

Rebecca added, "Another good thing about going in April will be the bird watching. There are so many different kinds migrating through there in the early spring—so Mom, be sure to pack your binoculars and bird book."

"Don't worry I'll put them in my pile of 'to go' things. Sounds like another fun thing we can do."

"Sure, sure!" Laura said, "And walking on the beach picking up shells—. Darn! Wish I could get a kid sitter. I'm getting jealous just thinking about all that."

I gave her a big hug and said, "Sweetie, we will definitely miss you but I PROMISE, you will be in on our next adventure."

After months of planning and research, Rebecca and I were ready for a fun time in the South Padre Island area. Everything went smoothly, from the short flight to the Harlingen airport, then picking up a rent car and finding our motel in Port Isabel. It was really an impressive little port town. We hardly knew where to start when suddenly the answer loomed up before us—The Point Isabel Lighthouse! There it was, proudly standing on a high point of ground still watching the bay—and Its town.

Its pure white masonry tower with the top two sections painted black was a very striking picture against the cloudless blue sky. After taking outside photos, we climbed the steps to the lighthouse entrance where we were greeted by a lady with a friendly smile.

She said, "Hi ladies, welcome to the Point Isabel Lighthouse. My name is Rita, one of the volunteers. If you have any questions, I'll try to answer them. Oh yes, please read the safety precautions before you begin your climb. The next chart describes the interior and exterior with many interesting facts. For instance most everything about the lighthouse is original except the beacon light and the necessary repairs. The most damage occurred in 1865 when the Confederate army fought to regain the tower from the Union army. That was repaired in 1866, and of course storms and time in general cause problems. I'm happy to say it is in perfect condition now, and we hope to keep it that way. "

The lighthouse chart described the first open section with the balcony like railing as "the cat walk." This is where the supply room is located and also the best look-out area. The top section is the lantern-room where the once powerful third order Fresnel lens shone. I have no idea what that means other than it must have been very powerful to be visible for sixteen nautical miles, as the chart stated.

As we read through the long list of things not to do, Rebecca laughed and said, "Mom—you will need to control yourself, and it says NO swinging from the rails!"

"Oh shoot! I thought that would be fun—uh, like heck! Rita, she's the one we might need to watch—just kidding!"

We were all laughing as Rebecca gave me a nudge and said, "Let's get on with the show!"

"Okay give me time to 'eyeball' things in this lower level." My next thought was how small the bottom floor was since it appeared much larger around from the outside. I was reminded that was because the walls were made extra thick to add strength. Somewhere I had heard that space was left between the walls so the tower could breathe. Perhaps that would account for some of the ghostly tales about lighthouses. "Brrrr!"

It was pretty intimidating looking up—and up—at the iron spiral staircase. This would be my first time to climb one of these and I was ready for the challenge.

Rebecca smiled and said, "Well, Mom—what do you think?"

"Wow, that's a bunch of stairs!" I declared. "We are actually here!"

I doubt the lady working there had ever seen any more excited visitors than the two of us. Hope she didn't think we were too goofy.

Rebecca was already busy snapping pictures as she answered, "Yes, that's a double wow!"

Not that it was necessary but I casually mentioned to Rita, the hostess, that one of our reasons to visit here was that I was writing a collection of short stories with a 'ghostly twist' and wanted to add one about a lighthouse. If I take a little longer, it's not because I'm getting tired—just getting the feel of the place.

With a laugh in her voice, Rebecca said, "Yeah—right! I'm sure there might be some puffing taking place. Especially since you're carrying such a big bag."

"May be big—but not too heavy! Let's see: my camera, water, small sketch book, pencil, binoculars, billfold, lip balm and a little flashlight.

"Gosh Mom—I didn't expect an inventory—. Did you say a flashlight?" "Sure, you never know when one might come in handy."

The lighthouse hostess laughed and said, "You ladies should have plenty of time since its two hours before I close for the day. Sometime while you are here you need to visit the Lantern keeper's Cottage at the corner. There are more historical things in there. By the way, what other fun things do you have planned?"

"Bird watching and beach combing," declared Rebecca.

"Ditto for me—and—getting a super good seafood dinner... Oh yes, and a margarita."

Rebecca and Rita the hostess simultaneously said, "I'm for that!"

"Okay! Let's build up a good appetite and see what's up there. Rebecca, you first since I'll be slower."

I started counting the steps as I wanted to stop on step number seventeen. I had heard a legendary story about a seventeen year old boy who was found dead on that step. Strange as it sounds, sometimes I am sensitive to things like that. Never know when I might 'pick-up on some vibes.' Hmm—oh well not this time! By the way, this legend is most likely untrue because I asked some people who were very familiar with local history and they had never heard that tale—. However, a few other places in town were mentioned that had an occasional visitor of the ghostly nature.

"Rebecca," I called, "These steps are so narrow I don't see how those big-footed fellows who had to climb them kept from tripping."

"Well, Mom, just be careful," she reminded me.

I paused by one of the walls and closed my eyes to see if I could sense the presence of a spirit (their energy) from the past. (Excuse me as I occasionally get to my paranormal side.)

In a fleeting moment it seemed I saw (in my mind's eye) the face of a young Confederate soldier. At least it was a gray billed cap like they wore. It sat at an angle on his blond, shaggy hair. Pretty far out—but maybe it was just my imagination!

Rebecca called out again, "Hey Mom, are you getting tired?"

"No! I'm good—just checking something out. Don't worry. I'll meet you at the top soon." Actually I was enjoying every minute of the climb—seventy-five steps to be exact.

"Okay—take your time, I am. Bet we're getting some good and unusual pictures!" Just as I looked up at her, she snapped another and I paid her back.

The last two sections had metal ladders and were fairly easy to climb but were quite narrow. I'm sure in the 'olden days' it must have been quite a challenge to carry a lantern, supplies, and possibly a rifle with only one free hand.

Rebecca was already on the next level as I stepped out of the stairwell. She said, "This is just too neat! I'm so glad you got interested in lighthouses."

"Gosh, me too! Thank goodness you also wanted to come here and actually did most of the planning." We walked around the cat walk several times admiring the scenery and exclaiming about how beautiful the water was. In fact, the colors were a brilliant turquoise like the Caribbean Sea.

After fifteen minutes or so she said, "Mom—guess we should leave and check out a few more things. There may be some pretty birds just waiting to get their pictures taken. We can always come back tomorrow."

I agreed and we made our way back down the winding steps, thanked Rita, and told her we would most likely be back the next day. She walked outside with us and told us about another nearby museum with a good collection of historical things that she felt we would enjoy as well. We told her we would definitely check it out.

I noticed the attractive shops across the street and said, "I wouldn't mind taking a peek in them—if we find any extra time."

Rebecca remarked, "We'll just 'play it by ear—eye' or whatever. Okay?"

"Sounds fine to me, Rebecca.

The lighthouse lady said, "I need to go over to the museum for a few minutes. See you tomorrow—have fun!"

The next few pages will show how a fun day almost turned tragic—just by my spontaneous change of plans—and a failure of communication. This is a brief description of what took place.

I told Rebecca, if she didn't mind, I would like to go back into the lighthouse and do some sketching while she went bird-watching. I said, "Tomorrow I will catch-up on that for sure."

She said, "Alright, Mom, I don't mind. I'll pick you up in a couple of hours. Be careful!"— She drove off and I went back inside the lighthouse.

With a carefree feeling I climbed the stairs to the cat-walk; stepped out into the fresh breeze and found a shady spot to sit. What an awesome view, I say to myself. I centered in on an area that would show part of the two mile bridge where several shrimp boats were tied up to the dock. The brown pelicans were gliding in gracefully, probably looking for fish scraps—. This is an artist paradise—I exclaimed aloud.

I took a drink of water, got my pencil and sketch pad out, and blocked in a few shapes. After finishing that drawing (to a degree) I felt the urge to walk down to the inner part of the tower. Since the steps and landings are made of iron, there was really no comfortable spot to sit—but that would be okay for awhile.

Turning to a clean sheet of paper I looked around for something interesting to draw. There was still enough sunlight filtering down to see what I was doing—however, at this point I wasn't 100% sure of what I was doing!

I heard someone climbing up the stairs, someone with heavy boots on —I waited but no one appeared. However, I felt a rush of cool air like someone or something had rushed past me.

"Yikes!" I cried out. "What was that? Odd—very odd!"

A strange thought went through my head—or was it a ghostly whisper? Straining my ears and eyes I looked around for a visible explanation for what was taking place... There it was again—almost like a whisper—"I'm lonesome for my love." I shook my head hoping to wake up from this unwanted dream and rid myself of the detached feeling that was creeping over me.

A cold hand on my shoulder startled me back to reality! "My Lord!" I cried out—"What was that?" Perhaps at that point, I shouldn't ask—since nobody in the flesh was here but me! I needed to get out of here as fast and safely as possible.

I looked straight up and saw the beacon light had just started its rotation—but where I was it was quite dark. I squinted my eyes trying to make out my surroundings. That is when I heard the soft in and out sounds like someone breathing. With a shaky hand I searched in my bag for the flashlight—as I told myself to keep calm. Then I remembered it was natural for a lighthouse to make these sounds—if the wind was blowing just right—so I was told.

I wondered what time it was. If Rita or Rebecca had called out time to go, I should have heard them. I felt rotten as I gathered my things up. I'll bet Rebecca is super agitated with me for taking so long in here—and also Rita, the lighthouse lady.

Even if Rebecca had honked the horn I probably wouldn't have heard it. These tower walls block out the outside noises especially in the inner part—where I had moved to for my last sketch... Why? I don't know what possessed me to do that. Also why in the heck hadn't I noticed it getting darker—hmm, maybe I was possessed.

I had not worn my watch on purpose that day because we talked about going to the beach. Just then it 'dawned' on me to check my cell phone and call Rebecca. I frantically dug through my bag looking for it ... "CRAP!"—I realized I had unintentionally left it in the car. Well at least I had my trusty little flashlight. Thank God that worked!

I cautiously made my way down the narrow steps and tried the door—but no luck. My only choice was to sit and wait until someone figured out where I might be. How embarrassing! I declared aloud, "Embarrassing and scary!" I heard my echo repeat, "Eerie—eerie"

<u>Meanwhile</u> —unknown to me, the following had taken place. Believe me, I heard—and re-heard about it several times. This is how it was later told to me.

Rita had returned to the lighthouse—read a few chapters in her book, then decided since no tourists were there—she left twenty minutes earlier than usual.

Rebecca drove up a little before 'normal' closing time and saw that the lighthouse was closed. Not seeing me anywhere, she figures I had gone to one of the shops across the street.

Thinking to herself she said, "Wish Mom had just called on her cell to tell me that." She glanced toward the passenger seat and saw the cell phone and loudly exclaimed, "SHIT!— That does a lot of good!"

After circling the block several times she stopped at each nearby shop and showed my picture, with no luck. Though she thought it unlikely, she drove to the museum (also across the street from the lighthouse). This time she just described what I looked like and said, "I can't understand why my mother didn't just wait on the bench in front."

The lady at the main desk said, "Rita popped in here about two hours ago and talked about you two ladies... Nice things for sure."

A second lady said, "I hate to even mention this dear—but—maybe your mother hurt herself in the lighthouse and is locked up inside. I remember Rita saying that she always announces closing time just in case there is a 'straggler.' It seems your mother would have heard her— unless..."

The first lady jumped up and offered Rebecca a chair and said, "Sit down my dear you look a little pale." Then she turned and fussed at her friend. "Ann! You shouldn't blurt out things like that!"

Rebecca said, "Oh my Lord, that would be terrible! It never crossed my mind that she might be hurt."

Ann, the museum lady said, "It's time for us to close for the day so we can all go to the lighthouse and see if that's where she is—no need to call Rita since we have an extra key."

Minutes later they hurried up the steps to the lighthouse door.

Rebecca pleaded, "Oh God, don't let my mom be hurt."

I heard the flick of a key in the door and it flew open! There we stood face to face! Looks of surprise—then hugs and smiles!

"Mom—are you okay?" Rebecca cried. "Thank God I found you! I've been looking all over for you—what happened?"

"First off I'm just fine. Thanks to my flashlight I was able to see my way down from the top. Last question however, I don't know for sure what happened or how. Things still seem a little unreal."

"Why, did you hit your head?" asked one of the ladies from the museum.

"No but other strange things took place up there—so I'm definitely ready to get outside."

Rebecca put her arm around me and said, "Well Mom, I think I better put a leash on you from now on." Seeing the serious look on my face she said, "Not really! I'm sure there is a logical reason for you getting locked up in the lighthouse."

"No—not logical at all—but I'll try to explain what happened later."

I told a 'little white lie' as I said to the two ladies, "I was so busy drawing, guess I took a nap."

If they didn't know already there were possibly ghost in the lighthouse tower—I wasn't going to be the one to tell them. After my seemingly large 'goof-up'—they would think I was also a 'nut case.'

"Collect your thoughts, Mom, because I'm expecting some answers before this night's over."

Rebecca and I both thanked the ladies from the museum for all their help. We exchanged hugs and went our separate ways. Ours was to find a good Mexican restaurant and count our blessing that my 'episode' turned out better than expected.

I breathed a big sigh of relief! "Thank God that's over!"

Rebecca said, "Yeah, I know just how you feel."

First thing in the car I put my cell phone in my big bag.

After a bit we found ourselves in a small but neat looking restaurant. "Yummy! "Yummy!" I said, "Umm, what great smelling food!" We were greeted warmly and asked what we would like to drink? Usually I say water but this time we both answered at the same time, "Margarita!" We all laughed.

Rebecca said, "Man, that sounded like we were a couple of alcoholics!"

As we waited for our food I quietly told her about the things that took place in the lighthouse. "Nothing unusual happened until I had the urge to go down to a lower level—that part is sort of a blur. I do remember hearing some heavy footsteps and felt a burst of cool air. It seems I starting drawing something. The thing that woke me up or brought me back to reality was—a—a cold hand on my shoulder!"

There was a shocked look on Rebecca's face as she said, "Oh my Lord! Mom, you poor thing!"

I said, "We better not talk anymore about my crazy experience till we get back to the motel—people will be staring at us."

"You're right Mom. Let me see what you drew."

I pulled out my drawing pad and showed her the port scene I had sketched from the 'cat walk' area.

She nodded, "That's good! Bet you can turn that into a nice painting."

I flipped to the next page with no idea what might be there—if anything... "What is this—? A portrait—but I never draw people!" Yet there it was in my sketch book! How did it get there?

It was a portrait of a young lady with sad eyes staring back at us. From the style of her clothing, I would think that she was from the 1860's.

The hand writing beneath the young ladies picture was also totally different than mine. It said, "My Love" --- Nathan.

Rebecca and I were staring blankly at each other when the waiter came to our table. With a big smile he said, "Ladies, here's your Margaritas. Enjoy!"

With a serious tone Rebecca said, "We will need another 'set' after this!"

I said, "DITTO!"

******